MODERN SHORT STORIES

Editor
JUIS S. RITA VAS

JAICO PUBLISHING HOUSE
MUMBAI ● DELHI ● KOLKATA
BANGALORE ● HYDERABAD ● CHENNAI

© Jaico Publishing House

No part of this book may be reproduced or utilized in any form or by any means, electronic or mechanical including photocopying, recording or by any information storage and retrieval system, without permission in writing from the publishers.

MODERN GOAN SHORT STORIES
ISBN 81-7224-954-3

First Jaico Impression : 2002

Published by :
Jaico Publishing House
121, M.G. Road
Mumbai - 400 023.

Printed by :
Efficient Offset Printers
215, Shahzada Bagh Industrial Complex
Phase-II, Delhi-110 035.

CONTENTS

ACKNOWLEDGEMENTS (v)
INTRODUCTION (vii)

1. IT HAPPENS 5
   Lucio Rodrigues
2. IN A VILLAGE, GREEN AND IN BLOSSOM 9
   Alberto Menezes Rodrigues
3. HOME 14
   Nisha da Cunha
4. THE LITTLE FELLOW 16
   Lambert Mascarenhas
5. THE COCONUT TREE'S CURSE 22
   R. V. Pandit
6. THE BOAT 24
   Nisha da Cunha
7. WORD FROM EXILE 25
   Walfrido Antao
8. PINGOO 27
   Armando Menezes
9. BETWEEN TWO LOYALTIES 30
   Maria Alzira Mesquita
10. THE NOOSE 32
    Manohar Sardesai
11. STONE SOUP 35
    Nora Secco de Sousa
12. THE IMAGE OF GODDESS 39
    Laxmanrao Sardesai
13. THE LEGACY OF LOVE 42
    Laxmanrao Sardesai

Contents (iv)

14. STILL LIFE — 46
    Manuel C. Rodrigues
15. WHEN THE BELL RINGS — 53
    Datta Naik
16. THE HYPOCRITE — 55
    Datta Naik
17. THE GREATEST SHOW ON EARTH — 57
    Abdul Majeed Khan
18. ON THE FEAST OF SAN JOAO — 59
    Adelaide de Souza
19. A TALE WITHOUT WORDS — 62
    Rui Peres
20. THE PICKPOCKET — 66
    Filbert Pires
21. THE RENUNCIATION — 68
    Rui Peres
22. TEMPEST — 73
    Manuel C. Rodrigues
23. THE AESTHETE (A monologue) — 75
    Armando Menezes
24. THE FORSAKEN SON — 78
    J. M. Fernandes
25. THE ROOT OF ALL EVIL — 80
    J. M. Fernandes
26. PINKY'S MOTHER — 83
    V. Sivaramakrishnan
27. FEAR OF DEATH — 85
    Ravindra Kelekar
28. THE SLIP — 86
    Louis Gracias
29. ROSALIA — 89
    Telo de Mascarenhas

ACKNOWLEDGEMENTS

This collection owes its existence to the interest, effort and patience of not a few authors who had little to gain from it. Dr. Manohar Sardessai, Dr. R. V. Pandit, Prof. Lucio Rodrigues, Mr. Rui Peres, Mrs. Adelaide de Souza, Mr. J. M. Fernades, Mr. Manuel C. Rodrigues, Mr. Alberto M. Rodrigues, Mr. Sivarama Krishnan and Mr. Filbert Pires deserve our special thanks. To Mr. Lambert Mascarenhas we owe an even greater debt for going out of his way to help us. Above all, however, our thanks to Mr. Antonio Norberto Morais but for whose great enterprise in obtaining some of these stories, this book would have been far inferior to what it is. The Department of Information and Tourism, Government of Goa, Daman and Diu was most helpful and prompt — a rarity in Government departments — in supplying the names of some authors and some excellent photographs of Goa.

The Little Fellow was originally published in the Illustrated Weekly of India: *'A Word from Exile'* in O Heraldo; *Stone Soup, The Renunciation, The Image of the Goddess, The Legacy of Love, When the Bell Rings, The Hypocrite, The Greatest Show on Earth* in Navhind Times; *'In a Village, Green and in Blossom'* was published in a volume *Flor Campestre'* in Portuguese; *Home* and *The Boat* first appeared in Opinion; *Fear of Death* was published in a volume of folktales in Konkani; *Pingoo, Aesthete* and *A Tale Without Words* first appeared in Goa Today. All the

Acknowledgement (*vi*)

above stories were reproduced by kind permission of the publications or the authors concerned.

To all others who helped with suggestions and otherwise, but must remain nameless go our sincerest thanks.

EDITOR

INTRODUCTION

If you would learn about a land and its people, you could make a start by reading about them, visiting the land and meeting the people; or you could read some of their representative literature. Perhaps, these are complementary ways of approaching your task. The literature would lend deeper insight to the more superficial acquaintance gained through statistics and personal impressions.

Enough has been said about Goa over the years. It is becoming an increasingly popular tourist resort with people from all parts of the country flocking to it. Yet, from the Goans themselves there is little of real value about Goa available in the rest of the country.

To fill this gap, we thought of a volume of representative short stories which would tell something worthwhile about Goa and Goans — a kind of 'bio-graphy of the Goan heart', to borrow a particularly happy phrase from Prof. Lucio Rodrigues. The story writer is less bent on defending or attacking than the expository writer and more concerned to put on paper what he feels is outstanding in his experience.

As time went on, however, and this volume gathered shape, force of circumstance forced us to change its nature somewhat. We no longer claim that this collection is a representative one, mainly because it is so difficult to say what is representative and what is not. But we do claim that it is a varied and interesting collection as the reader will soon discover for himself.

★ ★ ★

To an anthropologist and a sociologist, Goa is as interesting as any other State of India. Perhaps more so, because of its peculiar historical circumstances which set it apart from India

Introduction

for centuries. The coming of the Portuguese four and a half centuries ago resulted in the imposition of one culture on another of a profoundly different nature. The consequences of the phenomenon were not uniform on the Goan population. Different sections reacted to it differently.

Some Goans accepted the ruler's culture wholeheartedly. They began to speak their language, adopted their religion and dress and eventually became what was later to be known as *'assimilados'*. Still, it is futile to pretend that they became culturally entirely Portuguese, just as it is futile to pretend that 'wogs' (Westernised oriental gentlemen) of British India were indistinguishable from Englishmen. The *assimilados* remained Goan, whatever their wishes. Another set of Goans reacted violently to foreign rule. They resisted tooth and nail the Portuguese cultural and religious onslaught, remained fervent Hindus and spoke mostly Marathi; having a deeply rooted kinship with neighbouring Indians, they cultivated it zealously. A third section, comprising mainly but not only the poorer people, let the foreign customs seep into their lives and mingle with their own. They created the rudiments of a new culture. Their music, their folk-tales, their proverbs and saws, their cooking, their architecture acquired a widely recognised distinctiveness. This section spoke mainly Konkani, followed both Hindu and Christian religions. There is still a fourth group of Goans, who finding Goa too small to fulfil their ambitions, left their land of birth in order to sail the seven seas in quest of adventure, romance and fortune. But while they wandered they did not forget their dear home. They paid it periodical visits, sometimes returning for good, their fortunes made or their hopes dashed forever. A large portion of this emigrant population settled in Bombay and most took to speaking English.

Each of these Goan types has its peculiarities, lore and mannerisms that easily distinguish them to the experienced eye. Their study is naturally outside the scope of this book but a glimpse into them is offered in these stories for the enjoyment and enlightenment of the reader. If the reader is a Goan and living away from Goa it may in addition, hopefully, quench some of his nostalgia for his native place. It is not suggested that every story contained here can be classified according to the types referred to above. Sometimes they are mixtures of two or more. Sometimes they are unclassifiable.

All four languages spoken and written in by Goans are represented here though not in proportion to their usage or output. Their selection was solely dictated by their ready availability and the limitations of the editor who is fairly proficient in only two languages, has a nodding acquaintance with the third and is blissfully ignorant of the fourth. For this handicap he apologises, but unable to circumvent it hopes all the same that the variety of moods, styles, attitudes and situations, which is wide, will make up at least in part for the shortcomings.

★ ★ ★

An extensive criticism would be out of place here, but a line or two of comments on some of the stories would help the uninitiated reader in placing them in their context more easily than if left to do so on his own.

A few of the contributing authors are well-known beyond Goa, even abroad — Armado Menezes, R. V. Pandit, Laxmanrao Sardesai, Manohar Sardesai, Alberto M. Rodrigues. Many of the rest deserve to be better known. We certainly hope that this volume will do them that service.

Manuel C. Rodrigues' *Still Life'* is a psychological story, its setting like his *'tempest's'* is Bombay. The latter depicts something of the dilemma which many a Goan emigrant faces. Both of J. M. Fernades' stories present additional facets of emigrant life.

'Fear of Death' is a typical folktale. Thousands of its kind, each with a moral attached, are narrated by grandmothers to the delight of their grandchildren. *'Pingoo'* is a legend and a ghost story — another one is the *Feast of Sao Joao* — the likes of which abound in Goa, forming an inseparable part of village life and

Introduction

affording some relief to the villagers' humdrum life. *'coconut Tree's Curse'* is an original story written for children, it also suggests how folktales are born. *'The Greatest show On Earth'* uses as background a favourite Goan pastime — cockfighting. *'A Village, Green and In Blossom'* is of the romantic variety and draws on Goan village landscape for atmosphere. *'Word from Exile'*, though short, combines satire, poignancy and gimmick (it is a puzzle, the key to which we present in a footnote to the reader who may be unable to find it on his own). *'The Aesthete'* is difficult to classify even as a story but we thought it we too enjoyable to be left out. *'Pinky's Mother'* represents a rewarding effort of a south Indian to identify himself with Goa. Prof. Lucio Rodrigues' *'It Happens'* plays on the Batkar — Mundkar relationships as does Rui Peres' *"A Tale Without Words"*.

Just before going to the press we discovered Nisha da Cunha's *'Home'*, which we reprint from *'Opinion'* along with the *'Boat'*. Their author is a professor of English, Gujarati by birth and married to a distinguished Goan advertising executive. She uses and intriguing style, economical on the commans, a fine wit and irony, specially in the first story, capturing with delightful accuracy some stills of Goan life.

Incidentally the light tone in some of the stories is a refreshing relief from the deadly gloom that pervades most of Indian writing in all languages.

Perhaps, after reading these stories the reader may feel that the short story has a future in Goa. He may feel tempted to contributed to that future. If he does, the greater purpose of this unpretentious effort will have been served. To him, then, is this volume dedicated.

Luis S. Rita Vas

Chapter I

IT HAPPENS
Lucio Rodrigues

APRIL. The Indian summer.

The village wells are parched. The cracked soil thirsts for water. The dry furrows await the seed and the cool rain. But the sap of life leaps up in trees and men, in mango and coconut, in *bhattkar* and *mandukar*.

★ ★ ★

It was early morning, cool and bright.

Leaning over the well-window Guilherme dropped bits of mortar in the water and idly watched the magic of the ever-widening circles and the sudden darting of frogs. He was young and alone, the son of a rich *bhattkar*, now home on his holidays from Panjim where he had been studying of the past seven years.

"God give you good day, Babasinh", a soft voice greeted him.

He looked up and saw a girl of his age, whose body could not be contained in the tight-fitting cotton-frock she wore. She placed two empty pots on the edge of the well and began uncoiling the rope. Guilherme looked at her figure fascinated, like a boy staring greedily at a ripe mango hanging high on a tree. She must have become conscious of his stare, for the lowered her dark eyes and fastened hurriedly the noose round the neck of the smaller vessel. Guilherme's eyes passed over her body caressingly... full lips and cheeks like ripe mangosteen... round tanned arms... and a high challenging bust...

She stepped on the edge with her bare feet and lowered the smaller vessel, standing at the corner with her legs apart, so that her things stood out in relief through the stretched skirt. She bent forward slightly to tilt the vessel and let the water enter through the neck. Dark oily hair, parted in the middle and secured tightly at the back into a bun. The neck of the frock lay open in the middle giving to Guilherme's eyes a glimpse of the apex of the dark hollow between the breasts.

The vessel filled itself with a gulp. catching the rope in her left hand she placed her forearm on her left thigh, bending lower, so that the neck of her frock gaped wider, revealing the dark curves of her rich breasts. The fleshy contours played hide and seek with his eyes as she dipped her right hand a whole length to clutch at the rope and gracefully hauled up the vessel arm's length by arm's length.

She emptied the vessel into the bigger one on her left and lowered it again.

Again.. . The water gurgled up to the brim of the bigger vessel.

Again.. . She removed the noose from the neck of the smaller vessel, scooped some water out of it and then heaved it up against her left hip throwing her left arm round its neck. She lifted the smaller one in her right and turned away from the well, sweeping a glance past him. His eyes followed her as she walked away with swaying movements.. .

★ ★ ★

It was coconut felling day.

Guilherme sat in the shade of a mango tree. The tall palms swayed like village maidens carrying waterpots on their hips. Gusts of breeze rustled arpeggios through the leaves, and the ground was beautifully decked with light and shade.

It was a sight to watch the man climbing effortlessly palm after palm and hacking down the nuts with his heavy knife.. . His dark body shone in the summer sun. The place was soon covered with leaves and nuts in hundreds.

It Happens

As the shadows of the palm trees grew shorter and shorter, the heat increased. Guilherme got up and walked towards the place where some girls were collecting the nuts and leaves into heaps. One of them was the young girls who had wished him some days ago. He watched her from a distance as she picked the nuts, bending her supple body, wisps of dark hair flying in the breeze.

"You must be tired, Babasinh", said Jaki Anton, the *mukhdam*, coming towards him. "It's so hot", he continued.

"Ago Filsu", he soon called out, "tell your father to drop two good green nuts for Babasinh. And get them here quickly". Then turning to Gulliherme he said, "The milk of tender coconuts is very refreshing. When Bhattkar Bab comes round he never misses an opportunity to enjoy this drink."

So the girl soon came with two green coconuts, and squatting on her haunches she hacked away the soft green husk of the two nuts. The inner nuts were big and round. She bored a hole at one end and the milk spurted into the glass as she titled the nut over it.

It was a delicious drink, sourish sweet, and as he drank he looked at her, Filsu, standing in front of him, half-shyly, half-challengingly, with the two nuts opened at the top. The thin kernel was soft and dissolved on his tongue like jelly, and the taste of her full lips seemed to be in his mouth.

"That's the store-room at the end of the *bhatt*", said Jaki Anton, pointing to a rectangular structure of stone with a tiled roof. "You can go and have a look, though there's nothing in it except some dried-up coconuts. I have to attend to these women who have come to buy leaves and nuts".

Refreshed by the drink Guilherme thought he would have a look and walked towards the store-room slowly.

He stopped for a moment on the threshold and then stepped in. It was dark, and at first he could see nothing, but gradually he saw a heap of dry coconuts rising up before him on the right. A few rays of light came through the air-holes in the walls revealing cobwebs hanging from the ceiling. The place reminded him of some of the dark vaults in the cathedrals of Old Goa. As he turned to come out, he saw the erect figure of Filsu at the door as in a picture-frame, a broad basket on her head, her bust heaving, her neck taut like that of a goddess. She stood still for a moment, her raised arms holding the basket on either side.

"Are you not coming out, Bad"? she asked.

He moved to the right to let her enter. There was little space within, for the heap of coconuts was sloping almost to the door. A strong intoxicating odour came in with her and filled the whole place. Some stray hair were stuck to her moist temples, and her wet armpits and back excuded sweat.

"Take care of the coconuts, Babasinh", she said.

"It's alright", replied, with something of a quiver in his voice.

A round bundle of cloth fell from her head and uncoiled itself at his feet. For a moment she stood breathing hard. A beam of light fell on her upper figure. The deep shadows of the lower part of her body heightened by contrast the surge of her breasts. She bent forward to pick up the head-cloth at his feet. Blood leapt fiercely in his hot body and in a moment he stepped forward and flinging his arm round her waist drew her against him. Her body was warm, and steaming. She shrank at first, but only for a moment, and turning up her wet face he kissed with an accumulated passion her thick salty lips and crushed her big body in his arms.

"Babasinh'", she entreated, trying to free herself. "Let me go. I must fetch the remaining nuts".

★ ★ ★

It was a dark, warm summer night.

They lay nestled in each other's arms on the soft bed of hay, between two haystacks, snugly wrapped in the darkness around them. The scent of jasmine and mogras in her hair mingled with

It Happens

the warm smell of hay. They lay as in a dark pit, and the sky came down to meet the dark crowns of the coconut palms and the stars twinkled among the leaves like monsoon fireflies forming a canopy of blue and black and silver. Not a leaf stirred.

And in the silence his body communed with hers in the language of touch, motion, taste, smell; feelingly, searchingly, insinuatingly; vibrating the skin into ripples of delight. The green garden of her virginal body blossomed at his touch and like a fond gardener her felt the beauty of the *abolim* of her lips, the roses of her cheeks, the full-blown dahlias of her breasts, the white lotus of her belly, the lily-stalks of her arms and things, the aralia and the dark flower of her groin.

And his pilgrim lips and fingers wandered over the map of her body, circling up giddy heights and burrowing into warm hollows, round smooth curves and overhard edges, dreaming over long undulating lawns, tripping over familiar paths, and slowly, sacredly exploring the dark secret shrine where dwells the mystery of Kama.

And as he explored, blood panted fiercely in his veins, rushing tumultuously into the main stream, and his limbs leapt with the leaping tide, and from the bent bow of his body flew the flaming arrow of desire, yearning for its target, penetrating like ploughshare into earth, till the gathering storm within him burst like the monsoon rains, watering the seed, filling, flooding, spending itself, and leaving in its wake a strange quiet, a peace, a repose of tired, fulfilled limbs.

And the stars in the sky twinkled through the palm leaves upon two children of Nature lying limp in each other's arms.

One sultry noon, late in May.

Three saried women, each with a basket on her head, were coming from the Friday fair at Mapuca, trudging uphill with bent bodies. They halted at the top and sat under a broad mango tree, refreshing themselves with water melons.

The first: "You have heard anything of Mari Consao's daughter"?

The second: (eagerly) "Which Mari Consao's"?

The first : "Bostiao's wife. The girl, I hear, is after big game."

The second: "Oh, that Filsu! The other day Paskin was telling me something about her, but I didn't take it seriously. (In a whisper, bending forward slightly). The *bhattkar's* son?

The first: (nodding) They say Jose Mari saw them together one night, and it seems they have been meeting very often.

The second : The Lord have mercy. What! things have gone so far as that! I always said that the girl would come to no good.

The third: Grown up girls should be married off. The girl is in full bloom and would hit the eye of any young man.

The first: But why should rats meddle with things of iron? Suppose anything happens, who will have to suffer?

The second: Our girls never think of that. They fall in easily and then they begin to cry. The feast of Pomburpa is not meant for the children of the poor.

The third: If it falls on the ears of Bhattkan Bai, my Lord, she'll skin Mari Consao.

The second: Skin her? Why, she'll draw, quarter and salt her.

The third: Does Mari Consao know? Someone must warn her.

The first: Everyone knows. But she is a God-help-me-soul. The girl's been petted and see the result now. Girls should be branded when they are young.

The third: (Flinging away her melon rind and wiping her hands and face with the edge of her sari) Let's get along now.

And each taking her basket on her head, they proceeded along the hot and dusty road, homewards.

The shrill and angry voice of his mother awakened him from his day-dreaming. He dropped the morning paper on the chair and moved towards the door and listened intently. She was scolding someone. He went softly towards the place where the sound came from. A torrent of angry words fell on his ears.

"If you cannot look after you daughter, why don't you get her married?"

For the last few days his mother's silence had made him feel uncomfortable in her presence, and he had tried to avoid her as far as possible, taking refuge in books and papers. And now she was having it out. Must be Filsu's mother, he thought.

"It's always like that with you all. If we give you a little confidence, you take advantage of it and try to sit on our heads. You people have no sense of shame, and you think we too have none. No one will laugh at you. After all, you are toddy-trappers, and everything is the same to you. Why don't you send your daughter to Bombay? There are many loafers in the streets with whom she can go about, instead of running after people here. It's useless you weeping, I won't be taken in by any of those tricks. Send her away from here, or I'll drive you all out of my property. A *Kolvont* like her should be branded and shown round the village, naked, with a bull's skull round her neck".

Filsu's mother came out of the room wiping her eyes with the hem of her sari.

The next day Guilherme's father called him up to his room.

"I have a surprise for you, son", he said. You know, I always had a mind to send you to Lisbon for further studies, but your mother would not think of it. Now, at last, she has consented, and we have decided that you should proceed to Lisbon as early as possible. I hear there's boat leaving next month; and I am making the necessary arrangements. Aren't you happy, son?" asked the old man beaming.

"Yes, father", he replied, trying to look happy.

This was more than he had expected. His mother had taken swift and decisive steps to crush his vagrant passion. Lisbon...

Of course, he must meet her at once. She did not come to fetch water from their well the next day, neither morning nor evening. He slipped out of the house that night and went to their familiar meeting place, and waited. In vain. Two days later he heard that she had left the village, and no one knew where she had been sent.

Late that night as he lay in bed, memorise of the intimate night came to him mingled with the smell of warm hay, and the perfume of jasmine in her hair. She floated into his consciousness like a sensuous dream.

And now she was gone, leaving him a memory and an experience. Lisbon...

Chapter II
IN A VILLAGE, GREEN AND IN BLOSSOM
Alberto Menezes Rodrigues

In a lovely village, situated in that part of Goa which, years ago, was known by the name of Novas Conquistas (New Conquests) lived a farmer Tukaram Narvenkar, with his wife and three children.

Their house stood at the foot of a green hill, surrounded by lush cashew, tamarind and jumblum groves.

It was six years now since Tukaram had married young Leela, who had a dark wheat complexion, dark brown hair and lovely hazel eyes attended by fine eyelashes, also brown. The courtship had started quite early, when the two were neighbours, for the ancient house where he lived with his two brothers and her house were in the same *bairro* of another village.

They married, and two years later with the dowry money and his savings, Tukaram Narvenkar had built his new house, breaking away from his brothers because of frequent conflicts provoked by the irascible nature of his sisters-in-law. They did not regard with favour their sister-in-law who was beautiful and had brought in a good dowry.

And three years after the construction of the house, Tukaram acquired for tilling one of the paddy fields lying near the house as well as the cashew grove behind it, on the steep slope. Hills and valleys, streams and rivulets, cashew and coconut groves and greenery with variegated flowers gave the village a smiling look. The rivulets of sweet water, murmuring harmoniously, flowed through the cashew and coconut groves. Hindu women, mainly field hands with their tucked up clothes, used to wash their linen in them, accentuating the village's beauty, their lovely scenarios lending poetry to their rural customs and enchanting the passersby.

Leela used to washed her clothes in one of these rivulets. Often, the children used to go with her, one of them holding the infant brother only a few months old who loved fresh air and open fields. They used to lay a bed-sheet on the soft green grass beneath the branches of a *vonvouleiro* near the rivulet and on it they used to lay him. And while the mother was engaged in her work with her feet deep in water and her Kapodd tucked up, the children used to play on the green grass. Sometimes, they used to pluck wild flowers and fruits; at other times they would go after butterflies which, flapping their tiny coloured wings, travelled from bush to bush absorbing the nectar of the flowers. The younger brother would agitate his arms and legs in his bed, mutter monosyllables and enjoy looking at the heavens and listening to the birds which chirped on the branches of the *vonvouleiro*.

When the *vonvouleiro* was covered with flowers shedding a very suave aroma, *vonvolas* would fall to the ground. The children would pick the flowers and take them home to give them to their mother who, making a garland out of them would stick it to her hair.

In that home, life moved joyous and happy. Never a quarrel had broken the harmony of that house where love was deeply rooted. With her *choli* and *Kapodd*— the *Pallav* thrown expertly over the left shoulder—how lovely Leela looked! Animated by the certainty of her husband's firm love, she would throw herself, body and soul into the domestic chores, minding with love and concern the beings Providence had gifted her with. Jealousy did not even lightly touch her heart. There was no dearth of flowers in Leela's hair. And they were varied: flowers from the gardens, from the fields, from the hills; fiery *abolin,* milky *mogddins,* blond *vonvolas,* snowy lotuses and so many more; as many as are born in that beautiful bit of land called Goa! She liked surang immensely, these yellowish India flowers of captivating aroma which when threaded made lovely garlands. Behind the house hung hill flowers many of which she used, like the purple *pittkallin,* as purple as the *cucumb* on that beautiful dark temple.

Often, Tukaram used to bring flowers from the bazaar and he himself used to display them, affectionately around her strands. Leela was always greatly touched by this gesture of her husband and thanked him with a smile on her lips.

That year drought hit the paddy field and harvest was poor. A great sandness took possession of Tukaram Narvenkar; he saw the sepctre of hunger hit his home—"The *batkar* has to be paid the fild's rent. The baker will demand that I pay his bill for the bread supplied during the month. The milkman, if I don't pay what I owe him will proceed inhumanly; he will suspend the supply, little bothered that my children may come to starve.

"Where will I go asking for money needed to run the house? Who will lend it to me? Nobody. Two friends have already denied me this favour. Poverty is going to invade my home. How will my people live? My children, the flesh of my flesh, blood of my blood will starve.

"My wife, my dear Leela, plagued by hunger may curse the day she was united to me in matrimony.

"The *batkar* has reduced this year's rent to one fourth, for he was here once and saw the state of the corn. It is true he took pity on us since he told me to pay that one fourth after the harvest, after having sold the paddy. But where are the profits? The harvested rice I cannot sell because it is needed at home. He says he cannot overlook this reduced rent he having a numerous family—they are eleven children; and having no source of income other than his paddy fields."

—Why are you so sad and quiet?—Leela asked her husband, tenderly holding his hand—if the year was bad and the harvest poor, patience! Years will come which will give a bountiful harvest. Don't worry about what has happened. You have grown weak, that is what gives you these thoughts which do you no good. And after a pause:

—Come to the kitchen, sit by my side, while I clean the fish— And added smiling:

—You went to the bazaar and forgot to bring me flowers.

—I didn't remember to buy them, Leela, worried as I was with this misfortune.

—Misfortune? you are worrying for so little! But I am not angry with you for not having brought the flowers—Oh, far be it from me to be angry with you. No, don't imagine I am angry, for I said that jokingly, hoping these sad thoughts of yours would leave you. And tenderly laying her head on her husband's shoulder:

—It doesn't matter that you forgot the flowers. I know, for certain, that me you will never forget. And this certainty is enough for me.

Leela had noticed that Tukaram had been weakened a lot by a bout of influenza some days back and every morning after he washed his face, she fed him two eggs, anxious to see him well again.

Tukaram sits in the kitchen near Leela, who tries to distract him from that depression. But the companion's words do not comfort him. He thinks that poverty is inevitable and that misfortune is imminent; that quite a few mouths need feeding; that the three children are kinds and none is in a position to work in any house and contribute with his earnings to meet the expenses. Insomnia haunts Tukaram. He hardly sleeps for three nights. And thinks about suicide.

There was no reason for Tukaram to be so deeply disappointed. The mere fact that the year had been bad was not, evidently, reason to think of suicide. The husband of Leela suffered from weak nerves, for after flu, still convalescing, he wore himself out with harvest labour and his nerves were seriously affected. This ailment plus the shock of poor production generated in his mind the alarming obsession that a great misfortune was in the offing. That night, after dinner, Leela washed the plates and kitchen utensils and with a *ponntti* in one hand and a match box in the other made for the room where her husband and one of the children slept. she placed two objects on the floor, by the side of the mattress unfolded near where the husband lay and where the youngest son slept. She positioned herself before a framed Krishna hung on the wall and topped by a garland of artificial flowers and with folded hands offered prayer. Then she shed the *choli*, wrapping her bust with the *Kapodd's pallav* and she lay down by the side of the son, on the mattress. After an hour or so, in the silence of the night, she has the impression that somebody is weeping. She strikes a match, lights a *poonti* and looks at the husband and sees his eyes filled with tears. She sits by his side and caressing his temple and hair with the concern of a dedicated wife asks him the reason for his tears.

—The harvest was poor. Poverty will knock at our door. One day I'll go to the top of the hill and will jump into the Valley of Death.

—What are you saying!—exclaimed the woman in trepidation. You don't think of the destitution you would leave us in, if you were to commit suicide? You're young and got the strength to work with, and I also work whenever possible.

And in an affectionate tone, laying her hand on her husband's face:

—Try to get some sleep. If you sleep well, the thoughts that bother you will go away.

—No woman, your words don't convince me. My thoughts these days go often to the Valley of Death. I know the shortest way up the slope.

—Don't even jokingly pronounce so sinister a name. For God's sake don't talk about it again in my presence! I don't want to hear it! I get so nervous only to hear this name uttered.

★ ★ ★

The hill, on the other side, had a none too low slope; The hill was cut there almost vertically, and that was a rather high portion, and any one leaping below could not, by any means, escape the jaws of death.

Next to this hill stood parallel another hill not so high, both forming in between a narrow valley. And because some people had committed suicide hurling themselves from the top of the first hill into the valley, the latter began to be known by the name of Valley of Death.

Leela began to exercise vigilance. Next night after dinner, she stretched herself on the mattress by the side of the kid and kept a watch. It was a full moon night and its light penetrated the room through a glass tile, allowing her to distinguish the husband's body lying in bed.

During the first three hours, Leela did not sleep. But later, the resistance went on declining gradually, the eyelids descended slowly and she slept, beginning to snore.

"Leela has slept. Now I'll go to the hill-top." And Tukaram got up from bed, walked to the door opened it and got out. After a few minutes, the infant sleeping by the mother's side started to cry out in hunger. Leela opened her eyes, and took her breast to child's mouth and soon, still sleepy, raised her head and looked towards her husband's bed. Not seeing him, she was frightened. She lit the *ponnti* and looked for the husband in every room and when she saw the kitchen door open she took it for certain his having gone to the summit. she went out and there too did not see staggered, pulled at her hair and screamed. She was heard only by herself and her youngest son; there were no houses nearby and the other two kids slept soundly.

She took the path leading to the hill top. She climbed hurriedly the high slope afraid that she would be witnessing a tragic scene that would pierce her heart. She advanced through cashew groves, passing through wild undergrowth without fear of being surprised by serpents and jackals so late at night. She saw him finally at a distance of fifty metres.

—Tukaram! Tukaram! Tukaram! Stop. Tukaram! Where are you going?

The Hindu woman as a rule never calls her husband by name. But Leela, scared as she was, thought she should do it so that he may hear and see her more quickly.

The husband heard the voice, turned around and recognised her; but kept going.

The rapid climb of the slope had drained Leela's strength. Still, making a super-human effort, she walked—her fear had reached the climax since Tukaram had not stopped—but soon fell to the ground and lost consciousness. Fortunately Tukaram notice the fall having precisely at this moment looked behind to see whether she was still following him. the husband's love acted and made him turn back. He ran to the place where the wife was sprawled.

—Leela! Leela!—Now it was he who shouted. The roles had reversed.

Leela would not respond. In the moon light he saw on her face a trickle of blood and noticed that its origin was a wound on the right side of the temple. There was nobody there to help in this bitter predicament. He looked around nervously and discovered not far off a plant whose therapeutic properties he knew well.

He walked to the plant, plucked some leaves letting fall into his left palm the viscous sap that flowed out. Then, dipping the first finger into the liquid, went on to cover with it the wife's wound, and noted immediately that the blood had stopped flowing as if by magic.

The splendid result of the operation encouraged him and he murmured: This can't be death, a simple loss of consciousness. He tore off a piece of his vest, struck a match, burnt a portion of the vest and took it to his wife;s nose and shouted out loud— Leela! Leela! Leela!

This had its good effect; he heard a sniffle come out of his better half's mouth and soon she had opened her eyes. On seeing the husband near her a thrill of joy ran through Leela's body, she sat on a rock and asked the husband to come up to her. He assented.

—Why did you climb the hill? Why do you want to end your life? The mere fact that the rice production was scarce, is it a reason for suicide? What nonsense is this my dear! Am I not your wife to help in the difficult hours of our home? Don't worry at all if we should lack money. I shall know how to find it somewhere or other. The *nashnim* that we sowed on the hill will give us something. And then, the cashew will give us good revenue; don't you know the cashew nut fetches a good price, the same being the case with the wine?

This pathetic scene witnessed by Tukaram had impressed him profoundly. Pondering over the arguments advance by the consort, he began to regard the suicide he was about to commit as a piece of lunacy. Above all the questioning words of Leela echoed in his ears, showing him the insanity, the absurdity of his reasons for suicide; "The mere fact that the production of rice was poor, is it a reason for you to commit suicide?"

A marked transformation swept over Leela's husband. He saw that with that woman by his side, courageous ad comforting and whose arguments had quietened his conscience, he could perfectly conquer the crisis that their house was going to pass through as well as any other that might come to knock at his door.

He came still nearer to her and passing his hand smoothly down her neck, caressed it and her hair; made her rest her head on his chest; and his voice sounded in the silence of the moonlit night:

—You have been for me a saving angle. My love, you are right. For nothing I was going to commit suicide and to what destitution was I about to consign you all! I shall never again think of the Valley of Death. Never again will my lips speak these awful words.

Thus the black clouds which had darkened the sky of that couple's happiness, dispersed. The fall of Leela, unconscious and with the trickle of blood running down her face, had been the rainbow that dissolved them avoiding the storm that would sow misery in that home which their love had tenderly built in a green and blossoming corner of that picturesque village. She cradled her back in the broad chest of Tukaram. And in this position revelled in the good work that she had done and experienced a sweet feeling as it flooded her soul. Had it not been for her, her husband's suicide would have been consummated act, a bitter reality. A voice of singular beauty, of devine beauty, now sang inside her applauding her decision to climb up the high slope, alone, late at night, to save her husband from certain death.

They got up. And both now descended the moonlit hill, hands locked, and lulled by the sweet certainty that life would go on joyous and happy in their home, amidst flowers, laughter, love and hope.

Translated from **Portuguese**
by Luis Santa Rita Vas

Chapter III
HOME
Nisha da Cunha

AND once upon a time in a little village called Arpora there was a lady called Angela and she built a house near a small chapel and she built a kitchen and two large bedrooms and a large sitting room an a dining room and a room for the altar and the saying of prayers and a balcao to wait on.

And she went to Cuncolim in her carriage and that was many miles away but she was happy because the workmen made beautiful carved four-poster beds and chairs and tables and cupboards and they carved apples and pomegranates and animals and birds and they polished the carvings so that Dona Angela could see her face in the apples and pomegranates and she was very pleased. And then she went to a hill called Guirim and got some beautiful basket work chairs for the little garden with four great pillars and great basket covered bottles for the wine and then she went to Bicholim and ordered mud pots to cook in and then she went to her mother's house and took a crucifix and statues of the Madonna and her child and St Francis and St Sebastian and St Anthony and put them in the Altar room. Then when the house was ready she carved a beautiful front door and a garden door and the front door key was large and hung by a red cord and the door knocker was a metal lizard and she thought of a lizard because a guide had once told her in Portugal that gargoyles help ward away evil spirits from the Churches and why not her house she thought. Then she realised that the windows needed shutters so they were made of sea shells cut square and set in wood and then the house was ready except for a lovely green parrot placed on the roof instead of a weather vane which would have been useless anyway because there was never even a suggestion of breeze in Arpora. And on Sunday she got into her carriage and went to Church and gave thanks for her beautiful house and prayed that nothing but happiness would follow all the people that lived in the house. Next door to her house was another beautiful house but the husband died and haunted the house and nobody dared to live there any more though smoke always came out of the deserted house. Then Angela got married and had four sons, Francisco, Jeronimo. Antonio and Fernando and they did not care at all for the beautiful house she had built for them. Except for Antonio he loved the house and said "I shall always live here and I shall marry and my sons will live here too." But the other sons said "As soon as we are old enough we shall leave here and this gloomy dark Arpora and we will never come back here." And when Jeronimo grew up he said goodbye to his mother and went to Portugal and never found peace, and Francisco went to Portugal and became a doctor and brought peace to some people and Fernando became a priest and went to Angola and became a prison chaplain and tried to tell prisoners about the pain of Jesus Christ at a time when they were uncaring of everything except their own pain and then Antonio went to Bombay and said I shall come back. And he studied hard and longed to returned to his own home but this took many years.

And Dona Angela stayed in her house and locked up the sitting room and the dinning room and lived in the bedroom and prayed in the Altar room and the carriage got rustier and rustier and the horses wandered away and the grass got longer and longer and the hinges of the gate got weaker and the shutters remained closed and dust hung everywhere and soon the bats came because they thought the house was empty, they never heard a sound from Dona Angela's bedroom. And one day when she had waited longer than anyone ought to wait, she gave up waiting and died and Marialena's father had her buried in the cemetery of Arpora.

And one evening when Antonio had worked very hard he was taken to a large beautiful house called Villa Rozario with a beautiful Acacia tree that leant into the top window and two chicoo trees and one wild almond tree and there were lots of carriages in the driveway chandeliers and a marvellous fruit punch for the young people and the daughter of the house was called Eugenia and she wore a wondrous white lace dress and pearl drop earings and played the piano and sang like an angel and all the chairs were covered with needle point done by Eugenia and Antonio fell in love but he was only a poor student and her parents said "No our daughter will marry a rich man" and so Antonio went back and hoped one day that he would be rich and could marry Eugenia. Then one day he heard that she was married to a fine rich doctor and so Antonio went away sadly to the wars, fighting many years in Africa till his hair turned grey, yet he said "One day I shall come back and marry Eugenia and take her back to live in my house in Arpora we shall have a fine life there and she can go to Church every Sunday in my mother's carriage and she can sit and sew in the garden like my mother." And one day years later when Antonio was 55 and Eugenia was 50 her husband died and Antonio came back to Villa Rozario and he climbed the stairs and knelt by Eugenia as she sat sadly by the window not sewing but staring sadly at the pale blossom of the Acacia tree and her hair was not streaked with grey and her dress was black not white lace and he knelt by her side and he said "will you come with me and live with me and be my love and though I do not have a fine white court by the side of the sea still we could be very happy. Will you come?" And Eugenia said, "Yes", and they got into a ship with 16 large trunks full of Eugenia's dresses and 16 hat boxes full of Eugenia's hats and soon they came to palm trees and white beaches and Eugenia was happy and free and then they moved further inland to lonely avenues of trees and green paddy fields and wonderful great white Churches and Eugenia felt happy and free and then they came closer to Arpora and suddenly the wind dropped and the earth was dry and the trees were small and gnarled and the houses were not so whitewashed any more and all the pie dogs of the world seemed to lie like shadows everywhere and Eugenia began to feel less and less free and happy. And then suddenly the carriage stopped and there they were at Antonio's mother's house and the huge gate fell on its side as they touched it and all the leaves of many many autumns lay in the garden and up the stairs and an old glove lay on the balcao and the key would not turn in the lock and Antonio called many times "Mama" and a small white cat wandered out through the leaves till a young girl called Marialena came running and said she would take them to where she was and they followed her to the village cemetery and there she lay in the ground—and her headstone read 'Here lies Dona Angela who died of long waiting'—she had waited so long for someone to live in the beautiful house she had built. And they swept away the leaves and placed a bunch of flowers at the grave and then they went back to the house. And this time the key turned in the lock and they went in Eugenia and Antonio. And they then just stood there and the portraits on the wall of a doctor, a priest and a man who had no peace stared down from the walls and the cob-webs lay thick everywhere and the cane chairs were all broken and the great cross beams were eaten by white ants and the mattresses had fistfuls of silk cotton falling out and the Madonna looked much sadder and could barely bear the weight of her son and all the saints' wounds gaped wider than before and Christ on the cross sagged with the weight of pain and years and great bats flew everywhere. And Eugenia sat down and said "I cannot live here it will be like dying"—and Antonio sat down and wept and the small kitten came and touched his hand and he said "Eugenia you must do as you think best—but home is where you start from and I started from here. I shall stay here." And Eugenia got into the carriage with all her trunks and hat boxes and went away, but Antonio stayed in his house and cleared the cob-webs and mended the chairs and got rid of the bats and opened the shutters and cut the grass and swept away the dead leaves and washed the glasses and dug up the wine and lit candles at the altar and the smoke rose from the chimney and Antonio was happy. He had come home.

Original in English

Chapter IV

THE LITTLE FELLOW
Lambert Mascarenhas

THE Little Fellow sat in the grey sand in front of his little house. He was about five, with a mop of curly hair and a pair of bright and vivacious eyes peering from a face that Raphael might have given to Child Jesus. A visage like this in their own children would have sent the ladies of the village into raptures. In the Little Fellow, however, that face seemed to them ugly and unnatural, those eyes wicked and sinful. He did not know their opinion. He was happy as only children of that age are happy; his mother, grandmother, his home, the trees around it, and the red road being his world.

The toys he played with were a discarded reel, two coconut shells, four bits of tiles, two twigs and a yellow flower—dirty in the eyes of the well-to-do children, but to the Little Fellow his most precious possessions. When tired of playing, the little Fellow would carefully arrange these playthings in a torn cardboard box and keep them secure under the rickety bed on which he slept with his mother. As he played he sometimes would look up at the big ball that his mother called sun, or at the birds that merrily chirped, now on the guavas tree, now on the rose bush or on the thorny cacti that grew all round his house to form a sort of fence. Sometimes he lifted his head to watch the cattle as they passed serenely by his house with the young cowherd following them at a distance playing on a flute. The Little Fellow liked the tune he heard and wished he had a flute too.

The morning was beautiful as all days were beautiful to the Little Fellow. Only there was fire in the wind which smarted the boils on his neck and legs, making running painful. Yet, when he heard the church bell ring, the Little Fellow ran to old and broken-down gate which scarcely could be closed now. Made of bamboos it hung helplessly, on the short wooden post on one side, swaying in the breeze and looking like a drunken man. The Little Fellow hung on to the gate and began to swing to and fro as he waited, to watch the people from the church pass.

It was Sunday. But to the Little Fellow one day was as good as another. He counted time by the joy in his heart, by the love he had for everyone. He liked to hear the sound of the bell and watch the people dressed in beautiful clothes and hats walk down the road past his house. He loved these people, as he loved everything else—his mother, grandmother, the cows, birds, trees and his toys.

★ ★ ★

Slowly and rhythmically the people were coming up the road. First came that lady who always stared at him. She had a green dress today. He liked her very much. Then came a group of young men and young ladies, laughing and talking, who passed without looking his way. He liked them too. Then came the lady with pretty flowers on her frock, accompanied by her two little boys. They were nice boys and the Little Fellow felt he would like to play with them. They beamed at him, but the lady pulled them towards her and dragged them away. A little later came another group of boys and girls and they also passed without looking at him. And finally came that very, very beautiful lady who looked like the mother of Jesus, in the picture the Little Fellow's grandmother had on the wall. She had her little son with her today who wore a maroon corduroy suit and who, as soon as he saw the Little Fellow, began to run towards him. But the beautiful lady chased him and catching him held him in leash.

"Don't you go near him, he is not fit playmate for you." The Little Fellow heard her reprimand her son.

Just then a handsome gentleman with whiskers and a pipe in his mouth caught up with the lady and said to her: "Where does your little Carlos want to run, *Dona* Esmeralda? Does he want to play with the Little Bastard over there?"

The gentleman pointed towards the Little Fellow and the latter was happy that he was referred to as "Little Bastard". He smiled. This big word sounded nice to him, sounded better than 'baba' that his mother and grandmother called him by. He looked and looked at them until they passed out of sight and then he began to wonder why those little boys did not come to play with him, why those beautiful ladies pulled their children away from him. He puckered his brow and wondered and then his child mind understood that those big and rich people were really afraid of him just as he was afraid of the giant his mother told him would come and swallow him up if he cried. "They are afraid of me, hee-hee-hee," he laughed. It amused him, this foolish fear of grown-up people of a little boy like him.

His mother was washing the rice grains before putting them into the boiling water in the *burcullo* when he entered the smoky kitchen. His grandmother, sitting on the floor, a little away from her daughter, was pulling out with a needle a thorn that had entered the heel of her left foot. Running up to his mother and tugging at her dress, the Little Fellow asked her triumphantly: "What is Bastard, *mae?* What is Bastard?" He noticed his mother wince. He saw the skin of her forehead gather in creases. But without waiting for an answer, he prattled exuberantly: "That handsome man with a nice suit and hat called me that. I like him very much. I also like the lady who he told I was a Little Bastard. And that boy, he had such a shiny red suit today. I want to play with him, *mae*. I like him very much. You must also call me Bastard and you also *mamae*. Everybody must call me Bastard. I like it better than baba. I am Bastard...I am Bastard....My name is Bastard...."

He danced merrily on and on, hitting his chest with his chubby hands. When he again lifted his eyes and regarded his mother's face she was biting her lower lip; the muscles of her face were tightened and there were tears in her eyes. What had he done to make her weep? He really could not understand the elders. He also saw his grandmother violently withdraw the left leg from the awkward position it was placed and he knew she was angry. But why? The grandmother first glanced at his mother an then focussed her eyes on him. It was she who addressed him.

"That's not your name, Baba. Don't you listen to what people call you!" she explained. He noticed the harshness in her voice. "Your real name is Antonio, such a nice name too, but you are baba to your mother and me. Understand? Be a nice boy and now try to forget what that man called you, yes? You are baba, my baba, all right? Now go and play there outside with your toys, will you?"

Never before had he heard his grandmother talk in such an unpleasant tone. He knew that something was wrong. But what? He went out of the kitchen as he was told to. But he did not go far. He went near the window and listened. They could not see him. And then he heard his *mamae* scold his mother. He didn't like anyone to scold his *mae*. She was his mother and nobody else's.

"Disgrace!" he heard the old lady say. She spoke very fast. "You've brought shame upon me and upon this house. I've no face to show the neighbours and the rest of the people. That poor boy has to pay for your sins. Why didn't you drown yourself rather that come back and pollute this whole village? Drown with a stone round your neck, *hein?* I would have been at least happy in the knowledge that you are dead and not living with God's curse on your head."

The Little Fellow heard all, but understood little. What were the big words his grandmother was uttering? And how could she talk of God cursing? Did God curse, too? Wasn't it herself—his grandmother—who had told him God was good and loved all, even bad people? How could God curse then?

He raised himself on his tiny toes and peeped into the kitchen. He saw his mother looking intently into the fire. She was biting the nails of her right hand. Shi-shi-shi. Why did she do that? Hadn't she herself told him that good children don't bite nails? Then he heard her speak. "I told you I loved him very much.... we were to get married....Am I to be blamed if he was drowned....?" What was she referring to? 'Him. Who was 'him'? Was it himself she was referring to? He frowned, at a loss to understand what they were saying.

"It was all your father's fault sending you to Bombay and allowing you to mix freely with men," he heard his grandmother speak again. "A fine school teacher you became! Your father is dead and gone, and I have to suffer the shame you've brought on this house. Oh God, why don't you take me away from this world too, rather than let me face this humiliation!"

★ ★ ★

And almost as if God had heard her prayers, the old woman was struck with paralysis a few days later and passed away peacefully. Her daughter shed tears of remorse and tears of self-reproach for being the cause of her untimely death. But the Little Fellow did not know what death was. Because his mother wept he wept too; but soon after, he dried his tears and went out to play. He only knew love and he loved everybody.

When a few days after the funeral his mother told him that she must take him away, that they must leave the village, the Little Fellow puckered his brow and looked askance at his mother. "No *mae*, we mustn't go away from here." He began to plead with her. "This is a nice place. I like this house, the rich ladies, the little boys, I like everything and everybody. Don't let us go away from here, *mae*, don't let us go, all right? We mustn't go away, yes?"

He was given a little dog now and he showered on it the affection he had showered on his grandmother. He was happy. The rain that came either in a drizzle or in torrents held him spellbound; beautiful were the butterflies that flitted on the zinnias and on *mogras,* on marigold and *abolim,* and which he ran to catch and make his own. The rainbow fascinated him and he stared agape at the moon that rose at night and made his mother's tears glisten as she quietly wept in front of Jesus.

When winter came the village looked pinched and grey. The Little Fellow's teeth chattered all the time and the clothes he wore could hardly keep out the cold. His mother worked hard from dawn to dusk, and as she worked she coughed incessantly until one day she lay in bed in the morning and could not get up. The Little Fellow did not know what sickness was; nor did he understand what death was when she died a few days later. He looked at death with the same incomprehensibility as when it had visited his home before; this sleep beyond awakening puzzled him. As no one wept now, he wept not; he walked on tiptoes all the time. But when the priest arrived accompanied by six boys wearing white surplices and black cottas, one of them ringing a tiny bell, he was thrilled. Later when he saw men with red *mursas* and white *opas,* coming in procession holding candles in their hands he was so excited that he even forgot that they were taking his mother away.

★ ★ ★

That evening when they took him to the vicarage—the vicarage that was to become his home thereafter—the Little Fellow was puzzled. There being no one to claim him, no one to look after him, the vicar had taken the Little Fellow with him and handed him to the care of his cook. The Little Fellow watched the proceedings with awe, his new surroundings with great inquisitiveness. But when it dawned on him that he was not to go home that night to his mother he began to cry, "I want to go to my *mae.* I want to go to my *mae,"* he wailed. But when they brought his dog he felt happy and hugging it close, went to sleep.

Compared to his own little home, the vicarage was a palace,

a two-storeyed building, the upper floor of which was occupied by the vicar, the ground floor by the Parochial School to which the Little Fellow was at once admitted. There was wooden staircase leading to the upper floor, which the Little Fellow enjoyed climbing and descending. The floor was of wood and the Little Fellow, sometimes when the vicar was out of sight, jumped on it, enjoying the sound that it made, like the rumblings of thunder during the monsoon. But best of all he liked the church with its shiny golden altars and so many saints on them who, every time he went near them, smiled at him.

The boys in the school, ragged and dirty, the sons of labourers, fishermen and peasants talked and played with him.

They were not afraid of him like those rich boys and their mothers who had passed his house. When he told Agostinho who sat next to him on the bench that his name was Bastard, the son of the blacksmith looked at him quizzically and then whispered to him: "You mustn't tell lies, you know, God will punish you. Your name is Antonio, don't tell lies.

The Little Fellow shook the other's hand in protest. "Yes, that also is my name—Antonio—but that rich man called me Little Bastard that day and I like to be known as Bastard. It sounds nice.

"Which man called you that?" asked Agostinho.

"Oh, that rich man who passed my house with a nice suit and hat."

Agostinho twitched his nose twice, and then said: "Then I also like to be called Bastard. So if you are Little Bastard then I am Big Bastard. All right? I am bigger than you, am I not? So it's all right, yes?" And both of them smiled and continued scratching on their slates.

After school, the Little Fellow one day went across the meadow to the Portuguese Primary School to watch the boys playing there. He liked those boys with nice faces, clean clothes and plastered hair. Some of them were those who had passed his house when the Little Fellow lived with his mother. But when they saw him now they said to him in unison: "Don't come near us. You are a bad boy. Don't come here. You have no father!"

"I am not a bad boy, I am a good boy," pleaded the Little Fellow, trying to get closer to them. "I like you, I like everybody. Don't be afraid of me. I won't hurt you."

"Afraid of you" they jeered. They laughed in derision and then began to pelt stones at him, to drive him away.

Slowly and dejectedly the Little Fellow walked away from the playfield. He entered the church now completely empty of worshipers. The saints on the altars smiled at him but the Little Fellow was sad. He stood in front of the big image of Jesus hanging from the Cross, and folding his chubby hands said: "Jesus, am I a bad boy? Why don't you tell those rich boys that I am a good boy, that I like them, that I don't want to fight with them?"

★ ★ ★

For a long time the Little Fellow remained in the church. He liked to be there. he stood in front of each saint and spoke to him. He went round and round the church. When he was tired he sat on one of the benches on which during the Mass only the rich people sat. Then he climbed the four steps of the side altar and standing there pretended he was the priest saying Mass. But when suddenly the church bell rang the Angelus, its sound reverberating in the empty church and deafening him, the Little Fellow gave a start and began to run, afraid that the vicar might scold him for remaining out so late.

Surreptiously he wanted to enter the vicarage. But as he approached he saw at the head of the staircase the vicar talking to that beautiful lady with the face of the Mother of Jesus. On seeing him she said: "Here he is, *Padre vigario!*" pointing out to the Little Fellow with the forefinger of her right hand. "You had better convey to this contamination what I told you, *Padre Vigario!*" Then she said *"Boa Noite"* and began to descend the steps.

On seeing her from far, standing there on the steps of the Parochial House, the Little Fellow's heart swelled with joy. Had she come to take him? He had seen her every day in the church through the railing of the choir, watched enraptured her beautiful face and her beautiful clothes. He had asked God to make her and the other beautiful and rich ladies take him to their homes. He loved those ladies; he wanted to play with their children. This lady in particular he liked the best. She was very fair, and had many shiny rings on her fingers that dazzled like stars in the sky.

He had often wished she was his mother. How proud he would be of her!

When he noticed her pointing out to him and using those big words the Little Fellow was happy. Indeed she has come to take him. She loved him too, he knew. But when she began to descend the steps, he was disappointed. She was going away. Why? If he had only come back earlier he would have touched his hand to her beautiful dress. Why did he have to be in the church for so long?

He looked at her until she passed out of sight and then rang up the steps. "Did she come to take me, *Pad-vigar?* Did she....?" But when he looked into his benefactor's face he noticed it was troubled.

"Take you, where, my son?" The vicar shot a swift searching glance at the Little Fellow from under his spectacles.

"To her house, of course," the Little Fellow replied triumphantly. "I like to go to her house. I like that lady. I like everybody."

★ ★ ★

The vicar glanced at him, and then fixed his gaze on the garden outside where the marigold and zinnias, carnations and dahlias were a riot of colour. He fell into a deep meditation, his left hand in his mouth.

"Why did she come here, *Pad-Vigar?*" asked the Little Fellow after a minute or so of silence, unable to bear this suspense. "She wants me to go to her house tomorrow? Not today?"

The vicar, awakened from his reverie, looked at him. Simulating anger he asked, "Did you go over to the Primary School?"

"Yes, *Pad-Vigar*".

"Why did you go there?"

"To play with the boys. I like those boys."

"And what did those boys do to you?" asked the vicar, his brow furrowed.

The Little Fellow lied: "Nothing. They played with me. They said they like me, that I must come there every day.

"Did they?" asked the vicar. He did not believe the Little Fellow.

"Yes *Pad-Vigar*, they like me very much. But why did the beautiful lady come here? She likes me, doesn't she? She wants me to her house, no?"

★ ★ ★

The vicar narrowed his eyes and replied very slowly, "No, son, she doesn't want you to go to the Portuguese School ever again. She doesn't want you to play with the children there."

"No, no, she never said such a thing....No, no....She likes me. I like her....She is my friend...She is beautiful...." The Little Fellow prattled effusively.

The vicar did not know what to say. He had come to love the Little Fellow and was sorry for him. "All right, all right, she didn't say so, son, but I say it now. You mustn't go again to the Portuguese School."

"But why, *Pad-Vigar*? I like those boys, I like to see them...." Then he noticed the pain in the vicar's face and mistaking it for anger he asked: "Why don't you want me to go there, *Pad-Vigar*? Did God tell you not to send me there?"

"Yes. God told me, son. So you mustn't go, all right?" The vicar smiled and called out to the cook to come and fetch the Little Fellow for his dinner. When old Pedro appeared, the vicar was still smiling and he said to the cook, "What am I to do with this fellow, Pedro? What am...."

But before old Pedro had answered, the Little Fellow looked into the vicar's face with his beautiful eyes, and pulling the sleeve of his cassock replied: "You don't know what to make of me? No? Make me a priest. I want to be a priest like you....I want to stand in the pulpit there and tell everybody that I like them...."

"What!" exclaimed the vicar and began to laugh. "You, son of sin, a priest? Ha, ha, ha...."

By the window in the room next to the kitchen lay the mat in which the Little Fellow slept. Every night as he lay there, he looked at the blue sky and counted the stars, count them as only children of his age can count. One, two, three, five, ten, nine....Then he softly hummed the tune of a hymn or of the Portuguese National Anthem he was taught in the school. Tonight the sky was grey and the only one star he could see was soon wiped out by a big black cloud. He wondered for a while whether that cloud was like the mopper they had in the school to wipe out what was written on the black board. Then he began to think of the beautiful lady who had come to visit the vicar. She was a nice lady. He liked her. He also liked the name by which she had called him. What was it? Con....con....con....He could not even pronounce it. It was a big, nice name., Then he remembered what the vicar had called him—"son of sin". He liked that too. But what was sin? He must ask Agostinho in school tomorrow....

It rained torrents that night. The water entering through the open window drenched the Little Fellow's bedding, soaking him through and through. But he slept soundly, peacefully. When the cook went to wake him up the next morning, the Little Fellow was burning with fever. He was at once removed to the vicar's bed and the doctor sent for. The Little Fellow liked the doctor and also the bed on which he slept. It was a soft bed like the one on which he had slept at home with his mother. The doctor touched his chest with an instrument and it tickled him and he wanted to laugh. Only his throat was so dry that it pained him to do so. He also liked his new sensation they called fever. For now he could see his mother and she was talking to him....

On the third day the Little Fellow grew worse and on that Friday he died.

They buried him in a corner of the graveyard, without fuss or formalities.

And the rich and beautiful ladies whom the Little Fellow had admired and loved said that God in His Infinite Mercy had taken him away.

Original in English

Chapter V

THE COCONUT TREE'S CURSE

R. V. Pandit

(A story for children)

THIS story is thousands of years old. At that time the world had in it only two trees. One, a cashew tree, the other a coconut tree. The former was female, the latter male. They were sister and brother.

You could eat the cashew nuts with coconut water or you could eat the coconut's kernel with cashew juice and no man would ever need to eat anything else. His belly full, his thirst quenched, his stomach satisfied he could rest contented. No worries, no problems. Whenever he wanted he could eat, he could laugh and be merry with his wife, and he could sleep in peace. This was all he had to do. But slowly man became clever. Then this happened.

He learnt the way to make wine from cashew. His wife told him, "Don't, don't do it. God will be angry".

But he wouldn't listen. He prepared his wine: plucked a coconut from the tree, broke it, took away the kernel and pouring the wine into the shell began to drink. His wife felt miserable. That day she stayed hungry and wept her heart out. Since God had placed woman on the earth this was the first time she had shed tears. That was an evil and a much cursed day. This wickedness committed by man caused much pain to the cashew and coconut trees. Man, having drunk his wine, had fallen off at the foot of the tree. Seeing this and his wife weeping, the cashew tree said to the coconut tree: "My dear brother, what is this that has happened? What sin has that man committed?

The Coconut Tree's Curse

I used to feed him my heart's juice. But does this ungrateful creature not know anything about love? From my milk he has made poison and drunk it, and that too out of the vessel made with your heart's shell. Doesn't he know you are my brother? I cannot stand this. The time has come to tell him. My life is becoming unbearable. If this goes on I shall soon die."

On hearing this the coconut tree was upset. He said to his sister, "Kajibai, sister, don't be frightened. I shall bring that man to his senses."

Next day came. When man woke up, the cashew tree said to him, "Man, what you did yesterday was very wicked! But once is enough, please do not do it again. Were you not ashamed to make cashew wine and drink it out of my shell? Did you forget that the cashew tree is my sister and I her brother?"

His wife told him the same. But the instant the shellful of liquor reached his belly, he forgot his manhood. He yelled at the cashew tree in anger, "Shut up you coconut tree. Less of your boldness. I am sick of your coconuts and your sister's cashews. Now I only want that wine."

He thus reprimanded the coconut tree and repeated his feat the next day. "A shellful of cashew wine, likes that belly of mine." Thus singing he had two shellsfull. the third day three, the fourth day four, and the fifth day five!

All was over. This side his wife weeping away, hungry, was dying. That side the cashew tree was in sorrow!

At that time coconut trees were as short as cashew trees. Standing on the ground, man could pluck a coconut.

The coconut tree was after all a male, could it be expected to take all this without a fight? When man had drunk the cashew wine and had fallen off to sleep, the coconut tree said to his wife and to his own sister—the cashew tree, "My sisters, don't worry. I'll teach a lesson to this clever man. You will soon see how. Now the night is far gone. You sleep in peace."

After every one had gone to sleep the coconut tree asked

God, "The man you created has begun to drink; he's become a devil. From today make me tall. He should not get my coconuts. He needs to be taught a lesson."

God granted the request and made him tall. And He decreed: "For as long as man does not come to his senses, whatever curse you place on him will come true."

Another day began. When the cashew tree, man and his wife woke up and looked up, what a wonder! The coconut tree taking its coconuts had gone very high!

Seeing the coconut tree so tall, the cashew tree and man's wife were happy. At least now man will be sober, they thought. Man's face became purple with rage because he could not climb the coconut tree. He could not pick the coconuts, he could not get coconut shells to drink his wine in them. so he began to ponder how he would teach the coconut tree a lesson.

This side the coconut tree laughed with joy at his trick. In happiness it began to swim to and fro. The coconut tree had been very clever. He was now sorry for man and specially for his wife. And for their sake he began to throw down whatever coconuts they needed to eat.

The trick worked on man. When he was hungry he had to depend on the gift coconuts. He stopped drinking wine for a few days. He knew he could die of hunger if the cashew tree also went up like the coconut tree. For two days he sat quiet.

What went on in his mind nobody knew. "I must learn to climb the coconut tree and pierce his heart. I must make wine from his blood and drink it out of his heart thus causing him great sorrow,"—thus he was thinking.

The coconut tree began to be in friendly terms again with man. How much he had now improved. Man seemed to have repented. He seemed to have forgotten his anger. The coconut tree permitted him to cut wedges on his trunk so that man could tell his sweet tales to his ear. Thus he reached the coconut tree's ear. And having gone up he learnt to climb up and down fast.

With practice he learnt to pull himself up the tree with ease and stand firmly on the trunk by typing a rope to his feet.

Thus he was able to pierce the coconut tree's heart, to make wine out of his blood and to drink it out of the coconut shell. So wicked is man. Trees and animals, both have a good nature, but in devilish wickedness there is none to equal man.

The coconut tree and his sister were greatly pained. The greatest pain was man's wife's. But now nobody could do anything. Because, however high in the sky the coconut tree rose, man could always climb its trunk. There's no use going further up, the coconut tree now knew. He was angered by man's wickedness; and he laid this curse on him:

"You will make poison out of my blood and my sister's and drink it from my coconut shell? Well, drink it to your heart's content. May God bless you. but should you cause grief to the woman of your house, take care! I shall make you go begging with the same coconut shell".

Today, thousands of years later when it comes to begging, man walks about with a coconut shell for this reason!

Translated from Konkani
by Luis S. R. Vas

Chapter VI

THE BOAT
Nisha da Cunha

ONCE upon a time there was a village called Baga and there lived some fishermen and for years when they had worked hard for other men one day they were rich enough to buy some fine wood and leather and they built a beautiful boat. And they carved it and fitted it and sewed it and painted it and because of all the saints they loved St Antonio and they loved their boat very dearly they named it so even though they knew that their boat was a woman. And the boat loved the fishermen too and everyday they would set out at sun set and sail into the red of the sky and till the sky turned dark blue and purple and then black and the boat and the men would be all alone on the great sea which was sometimes their friend and sometimes not but they loved the sea and mostly the sea was their friend. And the fishermen would fling their nets into the sea and then they would wait and sit singing songs till morning came. And the boat loved the gentle rocking of the waves and lulled the fishermen because she loved them. And when the dawn crept up the mountain the sky would become grey and then white and they would struggle to draw the great nets in and the boat would hold very still to help the men and if the nets were heavy with fish the boat and the men were happy and if there were no fish or very few they would go back quietly hoping for the next day's catch. And at the beach all the men and the boys would gather and help to drag the boat up to the dry sand and the boat and the men would rest.

And this was the life of the boat for many years and she was happy to be so useful and nothing had ever happened to the boat except every now and again she would spring a small leak and

The Boat

her friends would stop it up with tar and the boat would go out as bravely as before.

But one night suddenly the boat was taken to a new part of the sea because they had not had a catch for three whole days and the sky was dark purple and so was the sea and the phosphorescence danced on the waves, danced like minute silver stars, appeared and disappeared, came and went, luring them on and on. And they were moving further and further away and a great wind had started up and the boat was tossed about like a little cork and the men struggled to keep her away from danger but they struck a great rock and the rock sent the boat so that it floundered in an agony of pain and thrashed about till it was exhausted and the men plugged up her wound with rags and bits of wood and the boat was brave and tried her best to make herself as light as possible and at dawn they somehow managed to get back to the beach and safety and they all lay down like the dead. But this time even though they got the best boat menders in the six villages famous for boat menders the boat could not be brought to life. And so it lay on the beach day after day under the sun and night after night under the moon till the sand lay on it heavy being lifted by the breeze all way and all night. And except for fishermen it was a lonely beach and the only building was a white house for priests to come to when they started getting sad about their lonely lives. And though the boat lay as if dead she was still alive but so sad and so lonely not to be able to be on the sea riding the waves.

And one day four grown up people and three children came down from a far away city to this little village of Baga and every day they swam in the sea and walked on the sands and the children first discovered the boat and they loved her and made her into their toy house and they played in her with cushions and sand pails and rugs and dollars and teddy bears and played there for hours. And the boat felt loved again but she knew that one day the children would go away and leave her alone again so she pretended not to love them very much. And one day one of the men who had a camera thought that the boat would make a beautiful film just the boat and its anchor and its oars and its beams and its name written proudly on its prow. And yes he thought this is a lovely boat and soon she will die and if I film her she will never die but will live forever. And so every morning when the sun was just right he came with his camera and filmed her with great care and gradually he came to love her so dearly that even the boat knew that she was loved and knew that she was still beautiful and now would live forever. And the man filmed her prow and her beautiful sides and her dusty torn nets and her name and her rusty pronged anchor and bits of leather and in the distance a boy played his flute and the man knew that the music of the flute would be just the right music for his boat film was sad and not sad, happy and not happy. And the man lay in the boat and felt the hard smooth surface of the wood and the boat felt the man laying on her and loved him and the two spoke to each other as only two people who love each other can and they felt that they would either of them never be lonely again having known each other like this lying together under the sky. And at last the film was ready and the man was happy but sad and the boat was sad but happy and she knew that even though she was old and brown she had been loved very much and this was enough and she did not feel lonely any more. Only a little bit. And the man went away back to the far away city and thought constantly of his new love.

Original in English

Chapter VII
WORD FROM EXILE
Walfrido Antao

You said to me the other day, dear reader, that in Goa literary criticism is not in vogue; that existentialism is decadent and atheistic; that Sartre, because he wears glasses is shortsight; that to be progressive is dangerous for the respectable parents of eligible girls; that real art or the 'nouveau recit' offends the prudery of the high moral values on which our well to do society stands. You told me more, dear reader, that in the current jargon what is needed is subtlety of the type 'to be a wage earner is not be under contract'; a spicy and local thing like 'the regedor of Pangarcem received a tip because the neighbour entered the kitchen of a married woman in the husband's absence'; a little story of love with bells tolling, candles burning, the maid servant weeping and the two together at the foot of the altar like two angles returned to earth etc.

Well then, dear reader, bound as I am by your cares here it goes as you order.

★ ★ ★

The story I am going to tell, dear reader, is as old as certain relics of old and familiar houses. It was narrated to me by one who today sleeps the long and calm sleep of eternity....She was a poor and humble woman. Husband, she had hardly had one. He had existed, yes, physically and socially and as the father of her children and as a name, a tradition. But the distance between the environments where they had lived, the culture of one and the initial pessimism of the other had opened a gulf between them.

She had lived alone in her world of housekeeping and dear memories of carefree childhood and an adolescence without horizons of a college of medieval tradition. Education she'd had but little; sufficient perhaps to understand from the start that the lie would haunt her like a ghost, that men are the followers of the law of 'might is right', of 'hemo hominis lupus'. Children her womb had produced without sin, but these, little by little, the college, the stormy sea of culture, other affections, other loves, other distances had taken them all far. And she had stayed there, quiet and good with a servant boy she had adopted of another woman, fallen angel in the ancient home, caressing the beads of a rosary worn out by so much ache and prayer. And then, one day, Death had knocked at the door of her heart now so panicky that it feared telegrams, thunder, a lightning. And death had taken away her man.

She had continued alone as usual with her prayer book and a nostalgia in the heart. Well, but she still had with her a magic talisman; a keepsake. A doll, a ring a diamonds, a rose on paper, who knows? The only possession of her heritage. But the keepsake, that is another story.

★ ★ ★

The world of the woman is a physiology, writes the enraged Honore de Balzac, frustrated in his 'liaisons amoureuses.' But Simone de Beauvoir, whom existentialism owes more than one philosophical 'experience,' in her *Second Sex* proclaims that woman is an autonomous complex deserving a place in the Sun and is not a mere savage conquest of man....and romantically his companion.

Ah! I was forgetting, dear friend, the keepsake, yes, she—the mother—had hidden it with rare care and concern. She was thus defending her own identity—her dream and tenderness, she held on to it as if to a last straw, in quest of an impossible salvation. The keep sake, a poem of a mother who had had no occasion to be one.

One day, day of sunshine and joy, the children returned. They were no longer the children of their mother, whom she had rocked in her arms almost fearful in the nights of the monsoons. No, they were men and women, their hair set 'garconette' style, the latest fashion in dress. They has ambitions, dreams, ideals. They lived rough lives, without fear of words. But she, the mother who hadn't been, was no more there. She had waited for years together for her children and one stormy night, a night of raging winds and rain, had closed her eyes to a world which had refused to accept her. The children came and took their places. Choosing freely. Each in his own way. One, a girl who wasn't any longer had embraced one who promised her love and fecundity. Another, a burly guy of 90 Kilos grew a beard and took to painting. The third one rose to be *'batkar'* and so forth. One night they decided to celebrate their return. With litany, sweets and crackers. And then one of them had the sudden recollection of the keepsake. They made for the box of surprise, which didn't even have a lock, of the mother who hadn't been. Some impelled by ambition, others by filial love and still others incited by the confused principle of "perhaps I shall get it!"

And the keepsake (secret, mystery, revelation) — there it was in the arena as if the children had been singing 'Mummy, I want'.*

Translated from the Portuguese
by Luis S. R. Vas

---

* (Refers to a Portuguese nursery rhyme which reads literally "Mummy I want|Mummy I want|a nipple"—Trans.)

Chapter VIII

PINGOO
Armando Menezes

....FOR example, there was that woman in our village, or just outside, who had unbelievable things happening to her for years. She had lost her husband at sea, or so they said—anyway he had never returned; and her children had left her, for no reason known to *me,* but there she was—an old wizened woman, with back bent till her backbone stuck out an inch—and if I remember aright, her fingers curved into a kind of talons like—a harmless enough little woman, though, who came to the back door sometimes, cleaning up what was left of a meal, though she never seemed to ask for anything. And she had terrible things happening to her at home—a small mudwall hut with a roof sagging under half-broken country tiles. She never cooked a meal but things started dropping from the roof—a sort of gravel or grit, right into the rice pot, or onto the stones where she sat grinding her curry. She seems to have cursed and borne it for a while, and told the neighbours; and they thought it was only an excuse for cadging a meal. Then things speeded up—the curry turned to blood—dark-red blood as when you stick a knife into a pig's throat; and then, her rice in the pot started turning to ordure. She seems to have gone on cooking for some time, dismissing the whole thing as a hallucination; but the thing happened again and again. I don't know how the neighbours got to know of it, for she, as far as I know, wouldn't tell—she was puzzled, or just dazed.

But things like that used to happen in our village—and I daresay in other villages too—and I have known people who had seen them with their own eyes. For instance, the whole village was haunted—I mean not the *whole* village, but there were spots, well-marked spots—near a boundary-stone, or an ancient tree, or the ruins of a once prosperous house, where you might see a ghost any night. And there were the *dadds* by day—colossal figures made all of air, who vanished only if you pricked your skin till it bled, or just stripped yourself naked.

It may be that today the law looks after boundary-stones, or the trees have been felled or simply died up and perished; but there is a sensible, almost a total, decline in the number of ghosts actually seen. A small child trudges to the grocery for a pint of coconut oil in the dark, alone. May be it goes to school by day; and they don't talk of ghosts in school any more— though they may be talking of the latest film star.

★ ★ ★

Still, the story I am going to tell you is true. It must be, for my father told it us, and he had it from his father, who was contemporaneous, or nearly contemporaneous, with what happened. Or it may be it was *his* father who had it at first hand. It's about Pingoo. The boy had come to the old couple almost by chance. They were sitting in their *balcaum* one evening to pass the time. It was a sure way of passing the time. People stopped at the gate and said, "Are you sitting?" or "Are **you** taking the air?", and they naively answered, "Yes, we are sitting", and so on; and then "How are you?" We haven't seen you ever so long—and how are the children? By the way, did you get any fish this morning?" and so on and so forth.

Well, one of those evenings, there was that boy who stopped at the wooden gate and shyly peeped through the bars. A short, plump boy, with a bronze complexion and an amiable face. He was not exactly what you would call handsome, but there was something about him, so to say, that made you at once take to him; a gawky sort of amiability. A likeable boy. He would be company, sure. So the old woman—who, coming as she did from a prolific family, felt the lonelier—hailed him. Come here, she said, and who are you? Are you from the other side of the ferry? I haven't seen you before And the boy, with the plump frame and the prepossessing face went into a rigmarole that would move a mill-stone. God knows what exactly he said. He must have said he was an orphan, and had not eaten a full meal for many days (plump as he looked), or that his stepmother beat him everyday; but the fact is, it all ended in the old woman asking him if he would stay with them. She even forgot to ask what work he could do. She wanted a son as well as a servant; somebody she could fight her loneliness with; her husband had his drink at meal times, and his *manilha* every Sunday—anyway, he could go out whenever he wanted....

★ ★ ★

He said his name was Pingoo. It sounded like a Hindu name, but he didn't say he was a Hindu; and he soon proved so smart and resourceful that they never asked him. Not even when he would not turn up at the family Rosary. Every evening, when the rosary started, they would hear the back door slam, and Pingoo was out. The old couple were hurt at first, but Pingoo was a gift horse—why, a very Godsend! He cost nothing but his food—and he ate so little of it, pecking at it like a chicken. And he was the very devil for work.

So good, indeed, that the old couple, marvelling at his promptness and his adroit ways, forgot to ask questions—even of themselves, let alone him. You had only to tell Pingoo to split some kindling, and there it was, piled up before the fire side, and they had hardly heard the noise of cracking logs. Ask him to get some fish from the *manos,* and he never failed; why, before the Rosary was half over, he was back in the kitchen with sparkling, quivering mullet—and yet it would be quite a mile to the *manos;* or, perhaps, did it just feel that far to *their* old feet?

And Pingoo was full of mischief too. The old lady had never seen a boy so full of pranks; not even her own boy, who had died on her at ten; and she grumbled at her husband's grumbles: "What did he expect a young boy like that, so full of life, to do? Stretch himself on the *balcaum* all day and puff at his *viddi?*" The naughtier Pingoo was, the better company she found him. The old lady felt as if twenty years had dropped off her back.

★ ★ ★

One day, Pingoo was sent with a message across the water to Saligaum. A married daughter had had a baby. It was a good distance to Saligaum those days. One walked the whole day, stopping only at the two ferries, slept off the tiredness and left early morning for home, with many hours of hot and dusty walking before one. But Pingoo seemed to have wings to his feet; he was back the same evening—quite early too—and never the worse for wear. An amazing boy! Had he gone indeed, or was it only one of his silly pranks, said the old man, puffing at his *viddi*. But Pingoo had, and here was the reply for proof. Pingoo was happy that he could show the proof. Or, what might the old man not think?

This went on for some time, until one hot May, the daughter came to Malar for the village feast, and the mango season, and the invigorating baths of the spring nearby. With her came her two children, a boy and a girl, both under ten, besides the baby. Pingoo was excellent company to them. He never slacked his household work; but he still seemed to have all his time for the children, who thought him a great guy. He would show them magic tricks. He would go into a dark room and shine all over: his eyes seemed large as saucers, and they glowed like a wildcat's. Once he picked up the baby and seemed to throw it up to the ceiling, and the baby simply vanished—or so it seemed to the children.

Their mother, being told, didn't seem to like it at all, not certainly, the trick of the vanishing babe. But she didn't ask questions. Her mother would be hurt; she had grown so fond of the boy. But she watched. There were no more magic tricks. The children, on the other hand, had already made friends with Pingoo, wanted him with them all the time—at play, at meals, everywhere. And, one evening, the little girl, who was well brought up and was naturally pious, missed Pingoo at the Rosary. She had never thought of it before; but today she missed him, she was becoming really fond of him. So, next Rosary, with her brother's support, she asked Pingoo. He jibbed. They rolled over him, seized him leg and arm and tried to drag him to the prayer-room, with its little shrine and the single *pantti* flickering some way from the smoky castor-oil bottle-lamp.

But they couldn't drag him. It suddenly came to them that they couldn't move him. He had grown unbelievably heavy. Like a rock. A magic trick! But when they talked of it at bed-time, lying drowsily on the bamboo-mat, their mother had a stab of doubt and did not shut an eye all night. Next morning—no use to tell her mother—she went to church as if for Mass; but her real purpose was to speak to the priest. They whispered together for a long time; and at last the priest was resolved.

★ ★ ★

The rest of the story is a little blurred. There used to be different versions of it. But the one my father repeated each time he told the story was that they priest came to the house in the evening—the house, you know, was one in that row that connected our village with Narvem, or almost. He seems to have come armed with holy water, and a lot of books. What *mantras* he recited we don't know; but the fact is that, at the first aspersion of the water, Pingoo, caught unawares, seemed to shrink and sag and wilt; he turned ashen pale, and at last, with a shriek and a flash of flame, vanished into air, leaving only a faint stink of brimstone behind him, and an old woman in tears, wringing and kneading her hands.

I don't know if I have told this story well, my father would remark at the end. But this *not* the usual sort of spook tale. It is history. And history has a right to be dull.

Original in English

Chapter IX

BETWEEN TWO LOYALTIES
Maria Alzira Mesquita

IT was 4 o'clock on Christmas morning. Isabel tossed in bed, fruitlessly trying to get some sleep; she felt herself physically worn out and naturally so after the running around she had done to keep everything ready for Christmas; the children, Joaozinho and Ana Maria, six and seven, vivacious and restless wanted *so* much! And Isabel was doing all she could to satisfy them on this holy night; she desired that the sweet joy of these moments should be like a very pure perfume which they could treasure for the rest of their lives.

In despair, Isabel got up, flung a coat on her shoulders and quietly walked out of the house into the garden.

The pallid clarity of the stars mingled with the soothing and mysterious light of her paper sisters, which could be seen over the verandahs of all the houses. A few feet away could be distinguished the white structure of the church in its simple majesty, the shadows projected by the mango trees, densely leaved, looked like delicate lace knitted by able hands; a light breeze blew swaying the foliage.

Isabel breathed in the delightful fresh breeze and sat on a bench. She shut her eyes and the memory of the previous year's Christmas surged tumultuously in her imagination; her frenzy had begun 15 days in advance; though she had to do all the housework, the servant having fallen ill, Isabel had built a beautiful crib, bought the gifts and prepared supper; and how lovely and well decorated was her table, full of appetising delicacies. She had felt physically tired, but how different was

Between Two Loyalties 51

that purely physical tiredness compared with today's moral exhaustion.

On that happy day Isabel was far from imagining that in a short time a scene which would last only minutes would destroy her small but happy family world. The details drew themselves neatly in her imagination; the arrival home of Pedro from his work, her presage that something grave had occurred, the talk with her husband.

★ ★ ★

Normally Pedro even if he had reason for worry always had a smile for his wife and patience to listen to the infantile talk of the kids; this day he had been different; he had not smiled, had absentmindedly caressed the kid's faces and had closeted himself in his room.

When Isabel took him the usual cup of tea Pedro said:

"Isabel I've got to talk to you" Isabel felt herself shudder at the strange solemnity of her husband and replied "My God say it fast, you are scaring me".

And then Pedro spoke; he related now he had overheard a conversation between two of his colleagues who were speaking of the self-interested manner in which Pedro had acted on bringing his father-in-law to his house; and Pedro, in a range, repeated the last words of the conversation: "That crook with all those disinterested airs is more cunning that we; he's brought the father-in-law to his house and certainly the old man will leave him his fortune which is enormous; naturally he justifies his action with the excuse that the old man has nobody to care for him; but I know this kind of saints."

"Isabel, you can imagine what I felt then. But after some thought, I understood that I was to blame; I had to know that in this world the rule is self-interest; why would I be an exception?

"And you, Pedro, you heard and still kept quiet?

"My first reaction was to sock them; but what would I gain thereby? Only that they be more careful in their talk; you think I'd convince them of the contrary? You're wrong; I might have won, but convince them ....that never". And then more decisively "Isabel you have to find a solution to this problem".

"What do you want me to do?"

"Take your father to his house, find out a capable and responsible person to take care of him and go and visit him as often as you can. I shall do everything within my reach to make the separation bearable, but it has to be".

On hearing these words, Isabel began to weep.

"Oh Pedro, you have the guts to hurt this poor man in this way? What does it matter what others may say if you have a clear conscience? You won't have to make the sacrifice for long. My father cannot live much longer."

"I see that you won't or can't understand my point, you ask me not to bother with other people's judgements, but you know me. You know that I don't have the patience and the philosophy necessary to bear an injustice. When I have a problem I face it and solve it; in this case you have to help me and the only solution is the one I have pointed out."

"I cannot agree with what you ask me" replied Isabel in a faint murmur.

And then Pedro said these hard words which still seemed to echo in her ears. "That's because you've no love for me; if in your heart there had been a bit of affection for me, you wouldn't talk in this way, but you never had any love for me, I repeat".

Isabel felt paralised and frozen on hearing these words. The words seemed to trample one another, such was the tumult of the feelings agitating inside her. Finally she spoke with a voice broken by emotion.

"I don't love you? And what are all these happy years which we both built with so much care? You think they would have been possible if I didn't feel anything for you?"

But Pedro wouldn't listen; neither did Isabel's pride permit her to show him the significance of those tears which she later shed.

And the next day, Isabel returned with her children and the father to her maiden house from where she had departed as a happy girl full of hopes in life and to which she was now returning a poor woman who saw the collapse of a happy dream into which she had invested so much care and in whose firmness she had the fragility to believe.

Translated from the Portuguese
by Luis S. R. Vas

Chapter X

THE NOOSE
Manohar Sardesai

It was impossible to live. Simply impossible. Whoever experienced such ceaseless nagging, such hellish noises, such baseless scolding! His house was a veritable pandemonium where life was a burden and work a punishment. He toiled the whole day long in his coconut grove, looked after the young palms, water with his own hands chilli plants and "eating-pan" creepers, kept away the cattle from destroying his orchard, and yet when he came home, all fatigued and sleepy, not a single sweet word, not a single welcoming glance! But hot words instead, words that scalded your ears like molten lead and pierced your heart through and through. He had been putting up with all this and much more for twenty long years. He was a rag, a blockhead, an idiot, a slave, a beast of burden, a coward who kept on living instead of dispatching himself to the other world. Why this endless succession of moral and physical miseries?

Why had he done today to deserve such biting, cutting language!

"Two days without fish! can you imagine that? And the river is so near. Pandubab brought to-day a bucket full of fish, and such nice fish! Oh! You will starve us all! You are not a man, no, you are not. You will see to-morrow! I'll go myself to the river with a fishing rod and then all the people of the village will say 'look that's the wife of that man who has no guts, who can't fish, who can do nothing but smoke day and night and grumble!'

It was too much for him. And his five children choking with malicious laughter! Why, why was he living! Death was better than all this.

Death! Dattoba startled; he rubbed his eyes and sat on the bed. Death! That was the only remedy; the only solution! Death was the only refuge from the harassing miseries of life! Dattoba's heart gently quivered at the thought of post-death peace.

But how to die? That was a serious problem; and the difficulty of suicide weighed upon him with all the force of eagerness to escape from this world. If men could die by just an effort of the will!

There was grave-yard silence around. His wife was sleeping in the adjoining room and his children lay huddled up in one corner. How happy they were, blissfully ignoring the miseries of married life!

Dattoba could distinctly hear the thumping of his heart from which life struggled to escape. So the last moment had come. He cast a parting glance around and with grim determination tinged with despair, went up to the window.

There was darkness outside. Trees looked like spectres, and house-tops looked like huge mountains against the bluish sky. It was the right sort of atmosphere for a silent suicide.

Dattoba pictured to himself the situation after his death.

How his wife would be wailing his death, how she would sincerely regret her haughty behaviour, her uncontrollable temper! And how everybody in the village would despisingly say: "Look! That is the woman who killed her husband!" That would serve her right!

And then he thought his wife might perhaps wake up and come out and seeing him at the window ready for a leap might entreat him not to jump down, might swear she would never behave in that way again but nothing would make him swerve from his resolve; jump he would even if a hundred men came to save him.

And he looked behind! There was nobody coming!

He looked down. He could faintly discern on the ground pieces of tiles and broken bottles. Dattoba could not bear the idea of those pointed broken bottles piercing his flesh; moreover the height was not much. He would not die on the spot; he imagined himself with broken leg bruised face and battered back, being carried into the house, with his wife venting her spleen on him and the children chuckling with laughter. No! That would be worse than death, and then there would be no means of getting out of it.

Dattoba felt seriously worried. Why the deuce hadn't his forefathers built a four-storeyed house! Surely they lacked foresight!

But he had it. He wouldn't give in so easily!

Why not jump into the well!

He did not know how to swim: and to be more sure he would tie a stone round his neck.

Like a man possessed, Dattoba went down running to the well. In a corner lay a stone looking expectantly at him. Just the type of stone he wanted. He lifted it and placed it on the edge of the well. But how to tie it round the neck? A rope! That what he needed now; and down he would go to the bottom of the well and then the next day there would be such a stir in the whole village!

Dattoba caught a glimpse of the rope hanging loosely over the pulley.

He pulled it. The pulley creaked; it almost implored Dattoba not to commit suicide. But nothing would break his resolve. He gave it another pull. But the rope would not come out. The noose obstructed its free passage.

The Noose

The noose! How did he not think of it! Death by jumping, Death by drowning—these horrible deaths never to be relied upon! Death by hanging! That was the surest way, the easiest method, the shortest cut to Death and eternal peace!

And the noose was quite ready to be slipped over the neck. He slowly pulled out the noose; made it as large as his head.

And now a beam was needed, a solid beam to support his weight.

Could he do it in his house? Perhaps his wife would wake up and then he would have to give up his idea.

A tree would be much better for the purpose. A few steps from the well, there was a mango-tree! But its branches were so thin and leafy!

Why not go to the nearby grove! Holding the rope coiled round his hand Dattoba slowly sneaked out of the kitchen-garden, taking care not to make any noise; but some dog lying in the street corner would raise its head and recognizing Dattoba, would go off to doze again.

Dattoba reached the grove. On all sides could be seen silhouettes cashew-trees, some high, some low, some wiry, some massive. He knew them all. He remembered how when he was young, he used to climb on them and devour ripe, plump cashew-fruits full of intoxicating juice.

Dattoba walked on and on through the grove, to find a suitable tree. Except for the chirping of "night-worms," and the rustling of leaves when light breeze passed through them, there was silence.

At last after five minutes of hurried walk Dattoba found a tree with two branches parallel to the ground. That was exactly what he wanted. Dattoba paused and then holding his breath, slowly walked to the tree that was going to be his scaffold.

In one minute he climbed it and was on the branch. He tied

the rope round the upper branch, with the noose hanging down. He carefully tested his work, found it well executed. He gave a sigh of desperate relief. He slipped the noose over his head, now he had just to let go the upper branch and swing himself forward; and in a few seconds, he would be as dead as those in the crematory.

The crematory! Yes he could see it from that height, its black door and high white walls.

Dattoba took a deep breath and said—"One, two—"

But before he could utter "three" he saw something that sent a shudder through his whole body.

It was a fire in the crematory. A ghostly fire red and green tinged with yellow! It was well-nigh mid-night: the gates of Yama's kingdom were being opened and soon he would see a macabre dance and hear horrible shrieks.

The idea sent a chill through his heart. But he wasn't afraid of ghosts! He wasn't afraid of Yama even, the God of death. Why should he then be afraid of ghosts, those creatures infinitely inferior to the Black Lord.

Yet his heart thumped within as a drum during "Shimga" festival; his body trembled as a withered leaf under the violence of monsoon blast.

One, two....

But what right had he to destroy his own life! Suicide was the vilest of all crimes, said the Shastras; and to defy the Shastras would result in his being turned into a monster in the next life and then be condemned to unbearable tortures in the kingdom of Yama. Dattoba pictured to himself all the breath-taking tortures—boiling in oil, sawing the body, pricking with sharp nails and the tortures he underwent at home would dwindle into insignificance before these.

But he was a man. It was his duty not to break the resolve. He was not a coward, a weakling, a doll of wax!

"One! Two!—"

Suddenly he felt something clasping on his arm; something fleshy, something cold and soft.

It was a serpent to be sure. That grove was infested with those terrible creatures. Dattoba's heart leapt into his mouth at the thought. He almost shrieked, let go his hold and came down crashing to the ground strewn with stones.

He passed his hand on his forehead. It was bleeding. Dattoba stood up. The noose from whose grip he had just escaped, stood dangling in the air. It was frightful; terribly frightful.

And fear took hold of Dattoba now, and he ran for his life, ran as fast as his legs could carry him, jumping over ditches and hedges, mounds of earth and logs of wood! And in a few minutes he was in his bed again with the blanket carefully hiding his face; and soon sleep crept over his eyelids and slackened the heavy thump of his heart.

Dattoba suddenly woke up at the voice so familiar but so unpleasant—the harsh, commanding voice of his wife. His whole body was aching, aching terribly. He felt someone was cruelly pricking pointed pins into his legs and ruthlessly hammering his head.

It meant, he was alive, alive to suffer meekly insults that would be heaped upon him, alive to live again the same sort of life, the life of a slave and a coward.

He opened his eyes. It was not quite daylight yet.

His wife's voice became more distinct. He hurriedly closed his eyes and waited for the impending doom. He heard her say to himself. "Where is the rope! Somebody must have stolen it. Those thieves have selected our house for robbery now. How shall I draw water now! I can't find any other rope."

Dattoba shuddered, he was the thief, the robber—and if she came to know about it, hard luck for him.

He threw off the blanket and rushed to the cashew-tree grove. The rope was still there, with the noose hanging down. He untied the rope, coiled it round his hand and came home. He stealthily went to the well passed the rope over the pulley and as he passed the noose round the neck of the pot, he thought to himself. "I shall put the noose round my neck, but shall never be able to tighten it. Never; never."

And behind, he heard the thunderous voice "Now go to the shop and get me a rope. Quick."

And as Dattoba sneaked into the house guiltily, he sighed. "Never. Oh. Never. I am a coward; a slave." And he wished he were dead hanging by the rope in the cashew-grove, the noose tightly closed round his neck.

Translated from Konkani by the author

Chapter XI

STONE SOUP
Nora Secco de Sousa

This is an old favourite Portuguese story, but with varying details. Sometimes the broth is made out of a nail instead of a stone, but boiled down the flavour remains the same and one which every thrify housewife will enjoy reading.—Editor

JOSE FRANCISCO BATATA FASTUDO was a seasoned tramp and globe-trotter. He was also a gay gallant who had travelled so widely that he knew the ways of the world and women as well as he knew the points of the compass. Consequently he got along famously with both. One late evening after having plodded all weary day with remote hopes of finding suitable shelter for the night, he saw a picturesque 'casinha' nestling amidst the nodding trees. There was a cosy fire burning within, and he thought longingly how comfortable it would be to toast himself before it and get a small something to eat. Just as he was pulling his tired and sore feet towards the cottage, the door opened and he saw an elderly lady advancing towards him.

"Boa trade Senhora, and well met!" said Jose Francisco Batata Fastudo in his most gentlemanly and gracious manner, at the same time bowing low and uncovering his head. "Boa trade Senhora," replied the lady who was fair, fat, and on the sundown side of almost fifty. Her name was Dona Maria Pulqueria Clementina Graca Torrada, and she descended from a respectable aristocratic family. "Where do you come from?" "North, south, east and west," said Jose Francisco Batata Fastudo. "As you see I have practically hitchhiked every inch of land under the sun, except for this pretty pin-point on the map."

"You must certainly be a great traveller then," said Dona Maria, "And what particular business brings you this side of the globe might I ask?"

"Oh! nothing special except my wander-lust to see new places and meet charming people like you. I had heard so much about the peace, prosperity, and plenty of the good things of life to be had for a song in Goa, that I always wanted to visit the spot. And here am I now, but without a roof over my head for the night," said Jose Fastudo tactfully.

"I had a sneaking suspicion there was something you wanted as soon as I set eyes on you, besides you have very taking ways. But you would do well to move away from this locality as fast as you can, as there are slender chances of you getting any shelter here. I am a helpless widow poor as church-mouse and my place is not a hospedaria," replied D. Maria.

"How selfish and sour you seem," said Jose Batata "but I do know that behind that hard exterior there beats a heart of gold. The Goans were always known for their lavish hospitality which is paralleled only by the proverbial generosity of the desert Arab. We are both human beings and we need each other's help in this hard world."

"Help? What are you talking about help, when no one has yet lent me a helping finger since my poor man's sudden death. Like the philanthropic soul he was, he contributed so generously to all the funds that now I am left without any myself. I haven't a morsel of food in the house and I don't know where I am going to get my night's supper. No, you will have to walk further and seek your board and lodging else where" emphatically stated D. Maria Pulqueria.

But Jose Fastudo was a persistent and persuasive tramp who had not in vain seen the world, and although the old lady grumbled and groused, she finally succumbed to his pleadings and said she would allow him to stretch out on the floor for the night, if he promised not to make a nuisance of himself.

Once Jose entered into the house he found that everything

in it indicated an air of refined taste and culture, and that D. Maria was not the destitute creature he had supposed her to be, but that the force of unkind circumstances had made her mean and greedy. In his most winning way he asked her for something to eat.

"Food? Where am I to get it from?" she said, "there is no bread-earner in this house and with prices skyrocketing daily so high for the bare necessities of life, such as me cannot reach or stretch for them. I feel hungry most of the time myself, but find it cheaper to starve."

But Fastudio was a clever fellow who had a head on his shoulders, and he set the little grey cells working. "Poor old mother," he said, you must be terribly under-nourished. It is time I rose to the occasion and asked you to have a humble meal with me instead."

"With you?" almost gasped D. Clementina, "what has a beggar like you got to offer me, I would very much like to know."

"He who far and wide does roam, sees many things not known at home," sang Jose Fastudo merrily. "Will you please lend me a cooking pot and a 'fugao' if you have one, mother?"

D. Maria was really very curious indeed to know what this statement meant, but before she introduced the vagabond into her spick and span kitchen she said to him "Senhor before your demands exceed my scant possessions I must make you understand that we no longer thrive in the ease and comfort of the good old days when food and drink were in abundance for all. This is now a new regime of austerity, where man must tighten his belt and learn to exist on freedom and fresh air alone. I have a casserole as well as a stove but the snag is the kerosene, as there is a big racket in black market rates going on these days for this essential commodity. Here is a bottle but count the drops you use."

Such difficulties however did not perturb Fastudo. Filling the pot with water he set it on the lit stove to boil. Then he took a round, smooth stone from his pocket, caressed it fondly three times in his hand, and carefully dropped it into the pot.

Meanwhile D. Maria stood and stared in stunned stupefaction, "What's this you're cooking' she asked?

"Stone soup" said Jose Batata as he solemnly began to stir the water with a ladle, with all the pomp and superior air of a culinary expert.

D. Maria had never in her whole wide and varied experience heard of anything in the shape of food being made in this way before, and she was burning with interest to know more. "That's something succulent for poor folks like me to know," she answered. "I would very much like to learn how to make it."

"You have only to watch me carefully to learn the art, "replied Jose Fastudo, as he went on stirring the mixture nonchalantly.

D. Torrada needed no second invitation and gathering her ample proportions she sat promptly plump near the 'fugao', her quick eyes following every movement of the tramp's hand.

"This particular type of stone generally makes good soup," explained Batata, "but tonight you might find it tasting rather thin, as I have been using this same stone for making broth for the whole week. Now if only I had a handful of "aveia" to put into it, that would make a world of difference to the taste. But since there is none, there is no use in wishing for it." And he went on stirring as vigorously as before.

"Well, if that is all that you need I will have to give you some from the new tin of oats I recently bought for Rupees three. In days of old the same tin used to cost Rupees One-eight" said old D. Maria in a garrulous and grumbling tone.

When she brought it Jose Fastudo dusted in some of the 'aveia' into the pot and went on stirring, while the old woman still stared fascinated with his doings.

This soup would be good enough to invite company for dinner," said Jose Batata adding another big handful of oats, "if only I had a few rashers of "presunto" and some cubes of

"Maggi" to flavour it. Oh well, that is only a lot of wishful thinking, so there is no purpose in indulging in such fancies."

"Meu Deus" exclaimed D. Maria "what expensive taste you have. It is such a long long time that I have seen either ham or Maggi cubes, that they are almost luxuries to me now. I did stand in a queue for five days on end to get a tin of Maggi but my poor feet got so weary waiting for it, that eventually my niece in Bombay sent me one which she bought on the pavement near the Dadar railway station for Rupees Fifteen.

Note well, the official price here was rupees 6.12. While she fumbled for her imaginary keys she mysteriously produced two cubes of Maggi and three thin slices of ham which she gave grudgingly to Jose Fastudo, who continued stirring the broth, while she sat nearer and stared as hard as ever.

"This soup is going to be superlative enough for a banquet," said Jose Batata "Caramba!" chirped the old lady and just imagine this wonderful broth being turned out in a twinkling with only a—stone.

"Now if only I had some "feijaomanteiga", some scrapings of cheese, and a drop of olive oil, we could ask the king himself to share some of it with us," the clever tramp said. "This is what he has specially prepared for him every night. I know, for I have many a time been assistant to the King's cook at Buckingham Palace." "Dear me, the King did you say? Well I never!" Nearly chocked D. Maria very much impressed and awe struck by Jose Fastudo's fine connections.

"But there is no use thinking about delicacies beyond our reach", said the artful tramp.

"Feijao-manteiga, cheese and olive oil are all the good things of the past" said D. Maria in a reminiscent mood. "But perhaps I may have some of these hoarded away somewhere for the proverbial rainy day. I will go and look for them." Saying which she hobbled towards her cupboard to fetch them.

★ ★ ★

Having got all he wanted for his soup, Jose Fastudo kept on stirring while his hostess took a seat nearer him and continued staring. Finally he removed the stone from the pot saying, "Now it's really ready, and we have a meal fit for royalty. Except of course that the king and the queen always had a glass of Portuguese port and a something extra special with kind of soup. And they always used a damask cloth on the table when they dined. Let's not however think about such princely things."

By this stage the selfish, and querulous, and discontented old dame was feeling quite grand and important herself, and she thought how fine it would be to have everything exactly as the king and queen did, for once in her life. She hastened to a secret panel in the room and brought out a bottle of port of ancient vintage and two glasses. She also like a conjuror, produced a roasted fowl the remains of a leg of ham, a delicious pudding, and some fruit. When she had set all these delicacies out on her best table cloth, it was really a feast fit for the gods.

Never in her whole life had the old skinflint had such a royal meal! Never in her whole life had she tasted such excellent broth. And just fancy, it was made with only a stone! D. Grace Torrada was in such high spirits and good humour at having learnt the art of brewing delicious broth and so cheaply too from a stone, that she was filled with admiration and respect for the vagabond who had taught her such a useful thing. They sat down together at the table and ate heartily and drank many a rousing toast to each other's health and happiness.

D. Maria Torrada become so loquacious and communicative, that she unburdened all her troubles and difficulties to Jose Francisco. "My husband left many accumulated debts which I have to settle" she explained "so that is one of the main reasons why I lead such a frugal and careful life. I have a small private income of my own but after all the taxes that are to be shortly imposed upon us are paid, I feel that I shall be left only with the taxes minus the income. Your company however has done me a world of good and cheered me considerably from my despondency. Do you by any chance happened to sing and play; I have my late husband's guitar and we could end the perfect evening with music."

"Forget all you worries lovely lady, for remember that nothing in life is so bad that it couldn't be worse" consoled Jose Batata, "Let us enjoy the memory of this incomparable night, and I shall sing a 'fado' called "Saudades" to you. And with the magic of music they beguiled the hours until they both became tired and sleepy.

★ ★ ★

Whereupon Jose Fastudo got ready to lie down on the floor for a good night's rest but D. Maria who had by now mellowed down to her most amiable mood, would not hear of it and insisted that he use the best bedroom and bed she possessed.

It seems superfluous to add that Fastudo did not need much persuasion. "It's just like the grand days I spent in the king's palace" he told her, "and I never came across a more desirable hostess in all my travels," He lay down his weary bones on the soft, clean, and comfortable bed, and was soon lost in the arms of Morpheus. When he woke the next morning, there was steaming coffee, eggs, bread, butter and cheese waiting for him on the table. And as he was leaving, the old lady pressed a fiver into his reluctant palm.

"Thank you many times over for the great lesson you have taught me" were D. Maria's parting words "I shall now live in comfort and plenty for the rest of my days knowing the art of brewing soup from a stone."

"There's really nothing you have to thank me so profusely for" replied Jose Fastudo "preparing stone soup is not difficult at all if only you have something appetising to flavour it with.

Personally I think the pleasure has been all mine to have such an appreciative and apt pupile. Adeus and God be with you always." Saying which he jauntily started on another lap of his journey around the world.

D. Maria Pulqueria Clementina Grace Torrada stood sadly in the doorway seeing the last of her good guest off. "Such clever and accomplished people are rare and one does not always have the good fortune of being entertained by them," the mused as she returned indoors to a house that seemed very lonely and dull with Jose Francisco Batata Fastudo, the versatile vagabond.

Original in English

Chapter XII
THE IMAGE OF GODDESS
Laxmanrao Sardesai

IT happened in the last century. In the village of Madkai in Goa there lived a goldsmith. Pandushett was his name. A gentleman he was, and a thorough one, simple hearted, scrupulous, religious and honest—a rarity among goldsmiths. For it is well known that goldsmiths cheat their customers. Now Pandushett never did anything of the kind. And people wondered at him. Not all of course, for there were some who made fun of him and his simple ways.

such was Pandusheett: ever self-contented, his eyes beaming with innocence and love; an image of goodness and virtue. Not that he was well off. In fact, he had to look after more than five members of the family, and guests would call on him invariably on all days. Whatever little money he got out of his work was thus all spent up.

Pandushett never worried about laying by some money. He was content with having just enough with which to buy food. "Do birds and animals care for the morrow? Why should one worry about the future?" That is how he thought.

When he went out for a walk with his fourteen years old sweet daughter, wearing a red velvet cap on his head, a long white coat, a clean dhoti and Poona-slippers, the farmers were happy and thought "Even a real Brahmin does not look as noble as this man." And indeed he was noble. He was entirely free from the village scandals and knew nothing about them. So sinless was his soul that his smile was like a child's. Never did he manifest any sign of anger, ever when harsh words were poured on him. He loved one and all alike.

He had but one madness—he was a great devotee of Navdurga, the village gooddess. He had full faith in her. He thought it was thanks to her that the village was happy and prosperous. No disease, no famine had ever touched it.

He was equally a lover of the verses of Tukaram and Diyaneshwar. It was only after paying a visit to the Goddess, and reciting some of the verses from the saints, that he did take food. Whenever there was some illness in the house, or some other misfortune, he did not fail to ask for the Goddess' help.

In the evening he used to go to the temple with his daughter Gauri. He would fix his gaze on the face of the Goddess and return home, his heart laden with contentment.

When the villagers had to settle a difficult problem, they would ask for Pandushett's services. They would listen to his advice for they knew he was a man above suspicion, above self-interest.

His daughter was only fourteen years old. Like a delicate doll she was, and fair too. Tender and full was her body, so charming and sweet her smile that it would make one forget oneself. Her smile would change the whole atmosphere with a rare splendour.

Smart but kind, she had inherited from her father all the traits of her character. Her face was as kind as it was pure. Simple was her dress; a skirt and a blouse. At her sight one could not help thinking: if there were a Goddess in this world, she would surely look like this girl. When villagers saw this incarnation of beauty, simplicity and goodness, in sheer delight they would give her their blessings. Now, people thought that the Goddess

The Image of Goddess

Navdurga was always ready to help her devotees. When she appeared in dream to anybody, that was an indication that it was the turn of his destiny. And once she did appear in dream to Pandushett: "Offer me your daughter", she said.

Hardly out of bed, Pandushett began musing over his dream. What did the Goddess mean when she asked him to offer her his daughter? How could he offer her to Goddess? She was neither a flower nor a fruit nor an animal. He divulged his dream to his friends. He consulted Gondu Bhatji, the priest, who told him that this was the will of the Goddess. "Make an image whose face shall resemble that of your daughter I shall see the fortune favours you". All were happy at this order of the Goddess. Pandushett was happy too. He was indeed fortunate. Fortunate also was his daughter, that the Goddess should desire to have a face like hers. How proud did Gauri feel.

The news spread everywhere. The villagers visited Pandushett. For, in fact they had all been wishing for a long time to have a gold image of the Goddess, an image which they could carry about in a procession.

The very next day all of the villagers, great and small assembled in the temple-square. They discussed how they could collect about 60 tolas of gold. Wonder of wonders, a miser gave them his treasure that he had so far kept buried in a secret place. Another offered his jewels. The rest of the money was collected from the villagers. The very next day the gold so collected was entrusted to Pandushett.

★ ★ ★

Joy of a new kind filled Pandushett. He clad his daughter with a silken sari and put on her costly ornaments. And Gauri looked like a Goddess. When Pandushett saw her long, curved and dark eyebrows, her bright eyes, her delicate nose, he thought that the Goddess had bestowed on his daughter all beauty and life. He forgot himself as he contemplated her. He forgot also that she was his daughter. He had set himself on the great task of concentrating on her soul's beauty and express it in the form of a golden image. It was as if he gathered to himself all her vitality and poured it forth into the image of the Goddess. As days passed the image took shape. And strange to say Gauri began to get lean and lifeless. However, her eyes shone with a rare sad brilliance; she ate less and less, she cared for nothing. She would silently sit in front of her father and through her eyes offer him her soul's treasure.

Gauri's mother was aware of this change in her daughter. She was seized with apprehension. She took her to the village doctor. But the doctor found that the girl suffered from no ailment. Even then, she was given medicine. Yet there was no improvement. Gauri stopped talking or smiling. At the end of one month she became extremely lean and pale.

★ ★ ★

At last the Goddess told Pandushett in a dream that she had absorbed Gauri in her image and promised she would again take birth as his daughter. The father's heart was touched to the quick. for a moment he thought that he had taken away her life, but his faith was so strong that the very thought of the Supreme Will of the Goddess gave him a further impetus to complete the work with the same zeal.

The image was ready. The whole village gathered in the temple for the inauguration ceremony. At the moment of inauguration, Gauri who was at home joined her hands in prayer and fell to the ground lifeless, as if she had given up her life in order to infuse life in the image of the Goddess. Pandushett went home running. The whole village was present at the funeral procession. But had Gauri really left this world? No, she had remained in the form of a Goddess in the midst of her own people. She had become immortal. And in truth, the image of the

The Image of Goddess

Goddess that had been created in the image of Gauri resembled astonishingly the 14 year old girl that was no more. The Goddess shone forth with the same beauty, the same expression, the same smile and sweetness that belonged once to the girl. Villagers big and small were filled with delight. Devotees from far and wide crowded to the village to pay a visit to the Goddess, got her blessings and went back happy. Brahmins and Sudras, priests and farmers the cultured as well as the illiterate all felt themselves purified at the sight of the image. Even criminals joined their hands in prayer and felt gentle.

The following year the golden image was carried in a procession in great pomp. As the procession was going round the village, the palanquin that carried the Goddess became heavy, all of a sudden, as it reached Pandushett's house. The bearers unable to withstand the weight and go further, stopped on the spot.

The villagers knew that it was miracle. Pandushett offered prayers to the Goddess. Remembering the sacrifice of his daughter the villagers became sad at heart and their eyes filled with tears. At that very moment news came that the goldsmith's wife had just given birth to a girl.

Pandushett's family prospered in the course of time but the man led a life of an ascetic to serve better his Goddess.

A hundred years have passed, but even to the present day the descendants of Pandushett beautify the image of the Goddess with rich garments and ornaments and place it in the palanquin on the day of festival. When the palanquin reaches Pandushett's house it gets heavy all of a sudden. People place it down for a while. They say that at the moment the Goddess perspires and her clothes get wet, that her face blooms with manifold expressions, that her lips quiver as if to utter a word. The brilliance and sweetness in her eyes make her look almost human. We might as well say that the 14-year-old girl comes back to life again. As if held back by some secret bond she stays there for a while and then with great pains takes leave of her father's house.

If you ever happen to go to the village of Madkai, listen to the story that the villagers will narrate. Go and see for yourself the image of the Goddess and do not forget the sweet girl of 14 who sacrificed her life to live a life eternal in the form of a Goddess.

Translated from Marathi
by Dr. Manohar Sardesai

Chapter XIII

THE LEGACY OF LOVE
Laxmanrao Sardesai

It had just struck midday when my daughter informed me that a Brahmin had called and desired to see me. I hastened to the lounge.

Indeed, it was a Brahmin, and at the very sight of him my heart went out to him. He appeared weary and his countenance reflected harrowing distress, akin to that of a mother-less child, but his clear and unfathomable eyes radiated spiritual strength.

"I have just come from Colem," he said simple and softly.

"Indeed, I presume then that you have seen my estate."

"Oh, yes, and I have been so happy since then."

"How so? Hitherto nobody had anything good to say about it....only that it is barren and ungrateful."

"Alas, for the cruelty of men. The earth is never ungrateful, and your land is a honeycomb....it has no equal in the entire Taluka."

"You amaze me. Would it interest you to know that many refused to have anything to do with it....and still others gave it up as a thankless task? And of all men, you feel attracted to my land. Parched land. How I wish to see its sods turning."

"If you permit, I shall till it with these hands of mine", he whispered.

"You, at this age? Do you realize the difficulties?

Pain showed on his face, but he went on in a plaintive note: "My shoulders, it is true already bear the weight of more than sixty years and my head is now grey, but I still possess the vigour of youth....and an unconquerable will". And noticing disbelief in my eyes he hastened to explain.

"My entire life has been spent in the closest contact with the mother Earth and I am hopeful that in less than a year I shall turn your fallow land into a blossoming garden. I would be grateful if you would come with me to your estate today."

"I Will, most willingly. You have aroused my interest."

★ ★ ★

Within half an hour we were bound for Colem. The train rumbled through golden paddy fields crossed swelling streams fringed with coconut groves and climbed hills covered with lush vegetation. Now and then we could see in the offing the seashore, only to lose sight of it at the next turn.

And all through the journey the Brahmin went on talking in this soft tone only pausing to take deep inhalations of snuff which he carried in a pouch.

"What is your occupation?" I asked, to began some conversation, and he seemed to be taken aback, but went on slowly.

"My ancestors have always been attached to the soil, and from my tender years, I felt likewise the irresistible call of Mother Earth. I could at that age, tell exactly how many banana and areca nut trees our farm had. I could tell how many bananas there were in each bunch. In short, I was an inseparable part and parcel of our land.

"My mother warned me to become a Pandit. Yet those who seek fame become Pandit, I thought. I sought neither wealth nor glory, nor fame, I was wholly engrossed in my land. How wonderful it was! The water rushing in torrents from the mountains filled the canals, meandering through the farm land. From any end I could count the banana trees, the areca nut palms and the fruit tree planted in rows.

The Legacy of Love

"As I grew up my parents insisted that I should take a wife: but how could I having completely identified myself with the trees, offering myself wholly to the farm my only love, perfect and disinterested? It was not the prospects of good yield that tied me to the land. If I watered it with the sweat of my brow it was because it sustained me. Far from it life for me would be meaningless without devoting to my land. Fully occupied with the numberless chores of the farm, I was oblivious to the world. The farm was my world....nay my life.

★ ★ ★

"Perhaps you think me insane for loving the land as none else. Well, love is returned in the same measure as it is given. The trees spoke to me and I understood their moods, their fortunes and misfortunes.

"Are you sure that animals do not speak to us? Are you really convinced that children cannot express themselves to us? They speak indeed. When our heart goes out to them they understand. How do children live and grow up? From what do they derive their vitality their life blood? Not from food and clothing surely. The mother will tell you that it is her love that nurtures them. She knows. It is her love that is life giving without it everything withers."

"It is the same with land. Our care and our caresses are far more powerful than the best fertilizers tend a plant daily; water it with your love and your shall see it blossoming and at the same time you experience strange feelings of exhilaration. You grow from strength to strength and your ambit of happiness widens.

And the Brahmin mused in the same vein.

"I lost my father....and then my mother. Up to the age of twenty-eight the thought of marriage had not entered my mind. One day I fell ill. I could not bear the thought of my land being left uncared for. Moreover, what would become of my areca nut palms in case I died? Marriage was the only solution....my wife and children would live and grow up in an atmosphere of love and devotion to the land. If I could not leave behind me worldly possessions at the end of my days I might at least leave them, as legacy, this unending love. Did not my ancestors do the same? Indeed, they trod on this land for centuries. They passed away, yes; but the land they bequeathed to me is eternal. Does it not therefore behove me to pass on the torch to my children?

"So I took a wife, and eventually my home echoed with the joyful peals of laughter of new beings. Life crowded me with bliss, and my land with greater bliss still. And there were no two opinions about my land being the most rewarding in the whole of Goa. My farm was the symbol of kindness and generosity of our country.

"Days wore on blissfully, until I reached sixty....and they might be sixty days. But alas, one day an official called on me bearing evil tidings. The land no longer belonged to me. I appealed to the Court of Law, but to no avail....My soul seemed to have departed from my body. Life without land was impossible. My wife and children left the farm, but I could not tear myself away, and wondered aimlessly for three days and three nights amongst my trees like a madman. On the fourth day, however, forced to leave, I clung to my trees in farewell embrace and wept.

"In my despair, I rambled through the country-side in quest of new virgin land, and I found it in Colem. My heart seemed to burst out with joy at the sight of this black soil which begged me for help. It had a desolate look, akin to that of a damsel who did not know yet the joys of fecundity.

"I was drawn irresistibly towards it, I held a handful of soil and caressed it between my fingers; I inhaled deeply its scent, and fell into a reverie.

"I was again in communion with the land. Everything seemed to have wafted away my troubles, my old age. I felt the strong call of this land which hankered for human caresses. It was an answer to my prayers. I longed to create in this thirsty and arid land a new kingdom where flowers might blossom and fruits ripen. I longed to quench the thirst of its wrinkled furrows, and invite the birds to build their nests there. I could already visualize a tiny paradise......"

The Brahmin was still talking when the train stopped at Colem. We alighted and proceeded to my estate. The Brahmins seemed to be at peace with the world, while the desolate condition of the land filled me with distress. But my companion gambolled like a small child at the sight of a new toy.

"Can it be that he is not in his right mind after all," I wondered, I could not help laughing at his antics. How could be turn this rocky soil into an orchard?

★ ★ ★

Three years elapsed, and my own affairs kept me very busy, though at times I had a desire to see my estate again. Every year the Brahmin called on me with the rental, and renewed his request that I should see the farm.

On the fourth year, however, I noticed a great change in him. On handing over the rental he entreated: "Sir, I pray you see your land at least this once. I do no longer feel the same. My task has completely sapped my strength. I can already hear the call of Death."

His words made a deep impression on me, and on the spur of the moment, I decided to leave everything aside and accompany him. "Forgive me," I said "it up to this time your sacrifice did not seem to find a response in me."

A few hours journey found us again in Colem. On going down a hill, I noticed that my companion was all eagerness to show me his achievement like a mother eager to place her newborn in the arms of her husband.

On seeing us, the Brahmin's wife and four sons hastened to meet us, their faces reflecting the same unstinted joy, and their eyes the same love for the land.

"Shall we go round the farm?"—invited the Barahmin, and continued: "It would be difficult to assess the efforts which the farming of this land has cost me. There was neither water nor a roof to shelter us, you know. And water and men are the lifeblood to land. "When I dug the first canals in this hard soil, my joy knew no bounds at the sight of the soil drinking deeply of the first gushing torrents."

As the Brahmin talked we entered the banana plantation, and were immediately sheltered by a vast canopy of green, made up of long leaves of hundreds of trees, standing in long unending lines.

Time seemed to stand still, while we wandered through every acre of the farm, stopping at every spring and at every green and luscious tree. I ate bananas and other fruits which the Brahmin picked on the way and offered me. But more than anything else, I was so spellbound by his eloquence, tinged by his passionate love for the land, that I forgot we had been talking for two hours.

When I finally decide to depart, the Brahmin saw me off at the fence which bound the farm. My heart went out to him full of gratitude and admiration, on taking leave of him. This simple being, so ignorant and ignored, so oblivious to learning and to world glories had created a world. He had settled his debt with Mother Earth.

A few days later, I received a telegram summoning me to Colem.

As I approached my estate, I could discern a pall of smoke ascending the skies. I ran like a man possessed. And soon was to know that my beloved Brahmin was no more.

The fire had already consumed his mortal remains. I fell down upon my knees, under the strain of an emotion which could not be denied outlet. I walked slowly to the house, shrouded in silence. The entire household was bathed in tears of sorrow, and I felt so small before their grief, that I could hardly speak:

"From this day," I said falteringly "this land is yours, my children. It is a legacy of a great soul that tilled it, made it fertile, and died for it. Keep it, my children, treasure this legacy—the legacy of love for the land."

And the smoke soared higher and higher, spreading through the skies the sublime message of the Brahmin.

Translated from Marathi
by Leofredo Gouveia Pinto

Chapter XIV

STILL LIFE
Manuel C. Rodrigues

THERE was life in the garden where the Mali, humming on his rounds, sprinkled water on the plants blossoming with flowers. There was joy in the mango-tree, where the squirrels in a riotous mirth chased one another and disturbed the chirping of the sparrows. But in Mr. Feldon's dining room there was unusual quiet. It looked more like a museum than a room of the living. The waiter, in his unrelieved white clothes, stood like a statue in a corner, staring at the plates laden with fruits and the roses drooping in the vase. Mr. Feldon and his wife sat down to tea, without a word, like two unknown travellers on the opposite banks of a river.

Mrs. Feldon would not have minded this silence. But what would the servant think of it?

"Why don't you have a piece of cake, my dear? It's good, just try it. Quite good!" said Mrs. Feldon at last.

Her comment however did not have the desired effect.

"I think I should know by now what is good enough for me!" said her husband, and threw down on the table the book he was reading and left the room. When he came back, a few minutes later ready to go out, Mrs. Feldon was more cautious and showed some anxiety.

"Don't be too late, my dear. The nights are damp and will do you no good."

Mr. Feldon did not reply. He went to the garage, took his car out, turned round the Malabar Hill and stopped along the

Mrine Drive. He sat there for a long time looking wistfully into the sea, as though it had been waiting to give him a lover's welcome. Then, he remembered. Pulling out a notebook from his pocket, he looked for an address, and drove towards the suburbs. Near an old three-storied building he parked his Studebaker, climbed up the stairs, and knocked at a two-room tenement.

"Is Mr. Rego in?"

Mrs. Rego who went to open the door called out to her son.

"Come in, please."

The visitor was conducted into the artist's room, which was both studio and bedroom. In one corner of the room was a cupboard containing several volumes on Literature, Art and Music. On the table, by the side of the cupboard, were his painting materials and a bust of Padre Angelo—his first attempt in sculpture.

"My name is Feldon—Martin Feldon," said the visitor introducing himself.

"Take a seat, please," said Alvaro, offering a chair.

"Thanks. Is that work your?" asked Mr. Feldon pointing to a landscape on the wall.

"Yes, all those paintings are mine."

"It's a beauty! Done at Mahableshwar?"

"No, Matheran".

"Of course, I remember, Artist's Point, I think Isn't it? It reminds me of an equally beautiful landscape I saw at a friend's place in Venice."

He paused for a while, took a cigarette-case from his pocket and offered one to Alvaro.

"Smoke?"

"Thanks".

Mr. Feldon took a long puff at the cigarette meditatively, and blew out the smoke in slow continuous spirals. Then he suddenly got up and moved towards the cupboard, as though something was over-powering him which could only find relief in action.

"Mr. Rego you must be a great reader," said he.

"No, I don't read much. Just a few books that I like."

"I see you read the Bible!" exclaimed Mr. Feldon finding a copy in the cupboard. "And do you play the guitar too?" he asked lighting upon a volume on "How to Play the Spanish Guitar".

"Not much. Just a few chords," replied the artist. "Music and Bible are my chief sources of inspiration."

"Really! I think they are also a great solace for the troubled mind, and the sick heart," said Mr. Feldon. And turning round to the artist, he added with a haunted look in his eyes.

"My purpose in coming here, Mr. Rego, is to ask you to do my portrait. Would you do it?"

"That's my profession."

"I know. And it's a noble profession too. But the portrait I want you to make has to be of an entirely different type and maybe somewhat difficult. But I am prepared to pay your charges—whatever they are."

Alvaro felt intrigued. He did not know whether to take the remark as a compliment or an insult. One portrait could be different from another in point of technique and the colours used. But difficult! What did he mean by that?

"I hear", continued Mr. Feldon, "from a friend of yours and a fellow-painter that you are a creative and most original artist. I've been looking for such a painter, one who is gifted at once with a romantic imagination and a sense of reality."

He looked out pensively, far away, through the open window....

"Could you conceive me as a dead man, Mr. Rego? Or a dead man still alive?—That is, whichever way you prefer it?"

Alvaro was taken aback.

"I don't understand you," said he, betraying in his voice fear of an impeding murder, suicide or some foul play.

"Don't be afraid, Mr. Rego," assured Mr. Feldon. "I only want it as a present for my wife—just a gift on the anniversary of our marriage".

"As far as I know," continued Mr. Feldon, "My wife has no taste for painting. But she likes it because somebody else does. Anyway, I thought a portrait of mine would be a good gift. I'm sure it'll be great fun, don't you think so?" said Mr. Feldon, and laughed dryly.

"Will you do it, Mr. Rego?"

It was difficult to reject such an offer. The commissions he had been receiving occasionally were scarcely sufficient to provide for a decent living. And his drawings were more talked of than bought.

Alvaro promised he would do his best.

"Thank you," said Mr. Feldon. "I want you to make it something big. You know. The artist may die. And the person he has painted too. But his work must live. It must survive decay and Time itself and go down the centuries telling its own story....But that's no consolation to the artist, I suppose," said he shifting the trend of his thought. "Life enjoys its little ironies. And the world in particular seems to think it necessary that an artist must die before he can live. Isn't it?....Well, before I forget, here's my photograph," said he handing over to the artist a parcel wrapped in a brown paper "And you must keep it between you and the door post. You know".

There was a touch of bitterness in his soul as he put on his hat, pressed a hundred-rupees note into Alvaro' hand and made ready to go.

"I should like you to give me a sitting, said the artist. "It's not necessary really. I've got your photograph. But I should like to do a few studies of your face in colour."

"Sure! Now?....Tomorrow?—"

"Not so soon. I'll make a sketch first with the help of your photograph. It might take me a week or so....Let's see....Could you call on Wednesday after next? Say, at about 4 o'clock in the evening?"

Exactly at the appointed hour, Alvaro saw Mr. Feldon get out of his car and come up the stairs.

"I think I've done some good work for you," said the artist, as he directed him to his room.

"Already? Let me see it."

"Not yet. Just sit in that chair for a while, please. I want to touch up the thing a little."

Alvaro set the picture on the easel removed the palette from the wooden box and began squeezing upon it a few colours from the tubes.

"I see a certain richness of colour in your paintings," remarked Mr. Feldon, looking at a picture on the wall.

"Are you a follower of the Moderns?"

"Not exactly. We have a lot to learn from them, though."

"Of course. I forget that India has her own schools of painting—the Rajput, the Moghul...."

"That's true. But I don't believe in any schools as such. I think every generation must start a school of its own, if that's necessary at all. I believe in a—

"This side a little, please. No. A little more. That'll do...."

"As I was saying. I believe in a synthesis between the achievements of the old masters and the healthy innovations of the Moderns."

"Quite right. I like that. There are some fanatics, you know. I do not deny that an Indian in particular must, above all things, study the at of his own country. And we know how great it is— Ajanta, Ellora, Elephanta, the Buddhist Sculptures. But you can't ignore the immortal Michael-Angelo, Leonardo da Vinci, Velasquez; nor Monet, Picasso, Van Gogh, Degas, Gauguin. It is only by accepting both these worlds that the artist can create a vital art true to his own age. Of course, he must possess a sensitive soul and what is known as high idealism."

"Yes," said Alvaro. "But you mustn't forget that the artist is above all a craftsman, which I am afraid few of your moderns are. Besides, I think they lack critical insight in general. The ancient masters, who first broke away from tradition, had not only an unfailing sense of colour and tone-values but were consummate draughtsmen. Thatt's important. They knew the rules of the game and knew how to break them. That's how they were modern."

"O yes! I see...."

"Have you studied painting, Mr. Feldon?"

"Well, I had ambitions, you know."

"You really know more about Art than I do."

"Not all that, Mr. Rego. I can only talk about things. You can do them. There lies the difference."

"I like the way you say things," said Alvaro. "But you shouldn't talk so much, Mr. Feldon. You make me forget that I have to paint you a dead man!" And, dipping his brush in turpentine, he mixed the green with purple to give a high-light to the chin.

"You've got very expressive eyes, Mr. Feldon; and a very resolute chin."

"Have I? I suppose it's one of the traits in my character."

"Perhaps," said the artist putting a darker shade on the eyebrows.

"Why do you say that?"

"Because I don't think you put into execution every thing you feel like doing."

"What makes you so sure?"

"Just hold your mouth for a moment please....The transparent softness of your lips seems to be in direct contrast with your chin," said the artist painting the lips in Rose Madder to get the effect.

"Yes?—"

Alvaro did not reply. His mind was already wandering in the vast complexities of human nature—like the swiftly changing tints of sunsets, caught in one moment, lost in another. And against these backgrounds, there passed before his mind's eye portraits of Freud, Jung, James, Vorel, Lombroso, in their different attitudes and expressions.

"Well," he drawled out. "I suppose everybody has skeletons in the cupboard. And here's yours, Mr. Feldon," said he turning the easel towards him.

"Like it?" he asked, wiping his brush, with a piece of cloth.

Mr. Feldon recoiled at the sight. It was a ghastly transformation!

"Can I take it?"

"Not to-day. It's still wet. Besides, I want to work a little more on it when the paint is dry."

Within a fortnight the portrait was hanging on the wall of Mr. Feldon's dining-room, much to his wife's embarrassment and greatly to his delight. It was acclaimed as a most beautiful work of art, though horrible to look at!

"The artist much have been mad when he painted that," said Myrtle's neighbour to her who had come to tea. "To paint Martin like a ghost coming to haunt you, and offer it as a present on your wedding anniversary! What an idea! You should ask Martin to tear it off, my dear,: said Mrs. white authoritatively.

Still Life

Mrs. Feldon was hurt. Blood rushed up to her cheeks. Shame, anger and resentment choked her heart. But soon a bright idea illumined her face. Immediately Mrs. White left, she phoned up Dr. Franz, the psychiatrist, and gave him instructions to contact her husband without letting him know that she had anything to do with it.

"You may find him very difficult, doctor. And sometimes maybe you'll find him quite sober...."

"Ehem."

"But don't be misled. Of course, I wouldn't like him to go to an asylum, and that's why you must do your best—...

"Do you think you could help him, Doctor?....Yes, please, do so whatever it costs you."

"I've handled many such cases, Madame Feldon," said the doctor assuringly. "You leave him to me, ehem? Yes. Don't worry. Bye-bye."

Mrs. Feldon heard the last click that disconnected her, put the receiver down and smilingly walked into her room. She grew happier and lovelier everyday. Took it into her head to supervise the cooking herself. Went to the market occasionally and made some purchases—ties and handkerchiefs for her husband, and several other things for daily use. she talked to her husband in the sweetest words imaginable, inquired frequently if he wanted anything; and, on his return home, went forward to kiss him.

This went on for a few days, until one night Mr. Feldon returned home drunk and in a fit of temper. The unusually kind attentions of the mental specialist, were becoming unbearable. It must be Myrtle's doing, he thought. She was perhaps trying to give a wrong impression to the people. Yes. That's it. I'll see to it.

He staggered into the house, flung his felt hat on to the sofa and stared fiercely at his wife who, seeing him drunk for the first time, recoiled behind a chair.

"Come and kiss me now, Myrtle," he shouted at her, supporting himself against the table. "Why don't you do it, eh? Because there's no one to see you?" said he, pitching his voice to a screech.

He stood there very like his own ghost descended from the portrait on the wall. The wife, frightened and trembling, ran to her bedroom, banged the door behind her, threw herself upon the bed and hid her face in the pillow. Mr. Feldon balanced his steps to the cupboard, opened a brandy bottle, poured some into a tumbler and drank it neat.

"You are a hypocrite!" he accused his wife following her to the bedroom. "I could have killed you, but I won't. I won't dirty my hand with your blood. Nor will I kill myself—"

He rolled his eyes, felt tired, dropped into his bed with boots and clothes on, and was soon muttering in his sleep. A few hours later he shouted for water.

"Get up," he said and flung out his hand which struck his wife across the face. She jumped off the bed and, after a while, appeared with a tumbler. With a trembling hand she poured the contents of it into his mouth.

The shaded lamp hid the expression in her eyes.

The next morning there was confusion in the house. The servants were conversing in whispers. Mr. Feldon was found dead in his bed dressed as he was. The police were immediately on the scene. They took down the statements of Mrs. Feldon's and others.

The old and most faithful servant of the house narrated with touching simplicity all that he knew of his sahib, his dead parents and his memsahib. His statement was nothing but a profession of love. He had loved his sahib like his own child, said he with tears in his eyes. Nobody has loved more, he said.

"We are not concerned with your love!"

The inspector was angry.

"What we want to know is, did they love each other?"

"Why shouldn't they? They were married only a year?"

The Mali was the next one to be called up. Flattered by the fact that his views were considered so important he thought it safer and, with an eye to his future, more profitable, to speak better of the living than of the dead.

The circumstantial evidence went against the dead. The postmortem examination disclosed arsenic poisoning and, at the corner's inquest, the verdict of suicide was recorded.

"What a shock it'll be to his wife!" said the people talking of Mrs. Feldon. "To make a widow of a young girl, just one year after her marriage! Who'll take care of her now? Poor thing!"

"I knew there was something wrong with that man, right from the day he brought that horrible portrait," said Mrs. White.

letters of condolences poured in regularly from friends and relatives alike, urging Myrtle to take heart and not to think too much of the unfortunate incident.

After a few weeks an auctioner was called and Mrs. Feldon sold everything there was in the house at the price she could get. Whatever she could not sell by auction she sold to a *jaripurana*. This done, she distributed money to the servants who had been faithful to her. And then she was gone.

★ ★ ★

The April weather is usually sultry in the City of Bombay. In Mrs. Rego's kitchen it was almost unbearable. The coal in the *shegree* was burning for afternoon tea. The doors were closed and no light could get in except through a small window on the southern side, which was deliberately kept open. Mrs. Rego was seated in a chair, perspiring profusely and staring blankly at the wall in front of her. Her right side was lit up by a stream of sunlight which, shot through by flashes of red flames from the shegree, gave a golden tinge to her grey hair. Her son sat opposite her, doing her portrait. His studio was not the right place to work in. It received too much light from all sides, through glass-windows and broken shutters, thus creating a glare and converting the face of the sitter, as it were, into a glassbowl, shining on all sides and offering no definite plane for study. The kitchen, therefore, was the only ideal place though it came in the way of cooking.

Mrs. Rego remained sitting in the chair patiently, without moving and doing exactly as she was told. A few minutes back she had got up to feed the fire with more coal, just at a time when Alvaro thought he had caught her soul shining in her eyes. And now she was about to rise again. The kettle was whistling and puffing steam.

"No, please don't move," said Alvaro. "Remain just where you are....I am giving the final touches—A minute or two more and the portrait is done."

He had painted his mother's portrait for the Art Exhibition. The difficulty was to frame it. The wood had gone so expensive. The glass and the mounts too. He dressed up and went to the Chor Bazaar. Whenever he ran short of cash that was the place to look for things. He entered a secondhand furniture shop and selected a frame.

"You can take it sahib," said the bearded bori. "You can take it with the picture and the glass for five rupees. I've got another frame to match. If you like it, I'll sell both the frames to you for seven-eight."

When the second picture was brought down from the loft, Alvaro was amazed. However, he paid the money immediately and rushed home with the pictures. One frame he utilised for the portrait of his mother. He hesitated to use the other. It contained Mr. Feldon's portrait—his own masterpiece!—though now slightly damaged. But what is he to do with the portrait? He dare not be seen with it now. They said Mr. Feldon had

Still Life

committed suicide. Some suspicious persons might accuse him of murder. He cannot return it to the dealer either.

He plunged his head in the hollow of his palms and began to meditate.

"Living though dead; dead yet living?"

Those were the words Mr. Feldon had used when he had first met him to present his life, as it were, fixed in an immortal framework.

"Living though dead; dead yet living!

Suddenly his face brightened and with the fury of a madman he painted on it a still-life.

★ ★ ★

In December both the paintings were exhibited. The portrait of his mother were awarded a gold medal. It was not for sale. The still-life was highly commended and was purchased by an art-collector.

Mr. Roach was greatly impressed by the painting—its glowing colours and the modernistic touch about it. Though the price was prohibitive Mr. Roach did not hesitate to write down on the spot a cheque for Rs. 1,000. Evidently he knew what he was about and was so happy that he immediately telegraphed the news to his wife, to prepare her for the latest acquisition.

Recently Mrs. Roach had taken a dislike to paintings. She had been married only a few months. But ever since her marriage she had systematically avoided any picture being nailed up in her bedroom.

"I am not blind to beauty," she commented in defence of her aversion to paintings. "I love beauty, but beauty in—"

"Emptiness!" concluded Mr. roach. 'But this still-life, Myrtle" proceeded her husband, giving her no time to talk. 'This still-life is a fortune. Someday it'll be priceless. We'll hang it up in the dining-room."

"Not there, please. You may put it up in the hall if you like."

"The right place for the still-life is always the dining room, my dear," insisted her husband. "Why! don't you like those apples, Myrtle?" asked Mr. Roach persuasively. "They are so lovely—luscious, ripe and plump," said he pressing her cheeks between his fingers.

"Aren't they?"

"Those apples of discord?"

"Why do you always talk of discord, Myrtle? What are you afraid of?"

"I really don't know, Pat. But I feel a kind of presentiment that I'll never be happy. You know I never loved Martin. But now that he's dead, I feel more unhappy than I had ever been with him".

"You shouldn't", pleaded Mr. Roach. "The past is dead and you must forget it. We mustn't fill our present and our future with regrets. Tear the old pages and start a new leaf, my dear. The dead never come back to life. And I am here to take care of you now."

"Yes, I know it. And that's why I sacrificed my peace. But was it worth it?"

"Worth it what?"

"Nothing," she blundered. Then regaining her selfcomposure "Just a woman's fear, I suppose," she added and kissed him long on his lips.

Mr. Patrick Roach understood the gesture of silence and did not ask for explanation. He knew that Time alone would gradually wipe away the memories from her mind. But it was not possible for him to remain with her until her heart was completely at rest. He was a traveller and was usually away from home on long tours. Sometimes for days together, sometimes for weeks. During one such tour, he received a telegram asking him to come home immediately. His wife had disappeared without a warning. And no one had seen her. The C.I.D. who were informed confessed they could find no traces. He was puzzled. Why had she run away? Had she ceased to love him? No! he said. That could never be. Then why had she left? Kidnapped? Or had she—No! he said again. The suggestion of suicide could not be admitted. It was horrible.

He sat worried at the table in the dining room drinking hard and smoking continuously. The sun was setting. The air was unusually calm. His eyes fell on the still-life. It looked almost unrecognizable. Had anyone interfered with it? Or was he drunk? The insufficient light prevented his seeing the picture clearly. Soon, however, the setting sun climbed down a few steps clear past the branches of the cassias in front of the window, and threw a crimson flash-light on the wall. Mr. Roach put on his glasses to examine the picture. The Prussian blue that had formed the background had faded and the Madder Carmine on the apples completely disappeared. And in some places the paint had cracked and fallen. Mr. Roach was shocked at the devastation caused by sunlight and moisture and air, and blamed his carelessness.

He sat there staring at the picture, again and again, and as he did so he felt he saw the portrait of Mr. Feldon come back to life. He rubbed his eyes to make sure that he was deceived. But he didn't seem to be. A cold shiver ran down his spine. For the first time he found it difficult to meet anyone face to face. He felt ashamed of himself and looked out of the window to distract his mind. And yet the figure haunted him. A peculiar fear seized his being. Not the fear of death—death which is sometimes a deliverance. But an unnameable sensation voiceless, irrepressible, inescapable! He turned to the picture once again, and Mr. Feldon was still there, more alive now than ever. He saw him struggle out of paint and walk towards him—slowly, deliberately, nearer and nearer, until he felt the touch of cold hands round his neck. Mr. Roach closed his eyes, clung to the table and swallowed a lump in his throat.

Chapter XV

WHEN THE BELL RINGS
Datta Naik

The trees, small and big, bathe in the moonlight....Slowing flowing, the air moves the fronds of coconut trees....All of a sudden from a distance a sickly dog barks in a pitiful yelp....The sound echoes in the stillness....The owls fly from one tree to the other and like circus jesters remain on the branches topsy-turvy....

Against this background, Antushet sets out from his hut-like house....With a lantern in one hand and a stick in the other....Antushet looks all around....aimlessly....And then walks with his stick on that red soil path as if somebody pulls him ahead...Sometimes he stops under a tree....Takes a deep breath and while exhaling starts his walking....sometimes the wick of the lantern wavers....Antushet stops again....Trims the wick and walk again....with an ecstasy of his own....world of his own....reviving and revising his past life....

Yes....Antushet is suffering from lung cancer....Very often a muscle moves in his neck....that produces peculiar sound || gud || gud || .... At such times, Antushet stops for a deep breath....so many days have passed like this....this this....Right from the day the doctor diagnosed his disease....Antushet cannot speak due to this cancer....For a year and half. Antushet has to observe things, bad and good....without a word from his mouth....has to observe only....like a balance-minded yogin....pouring water of patience on the bursting fire of anger....

For the whole day, Antushet sees things....things happening in the present and awaits for those which may occur in the future....At night, Antushet sleeps rarely....Antushet sits down on his bed in the verandah as the Goddess Sleep delays her arrival....picks up his lantern....lights it and begins walking with the help of his stick....without seeing whether the night is dark or moonlit....bearing the revolution of thoughts in his mind....

★ ★ ★

....Antushet recalls his childhood....his goldsmith father he remembers....he, who was famous for his artistry and craftsmanship....Like a larva turning into a beautiful butterfly with its knowledge Antushet had found himself turned into a young man....he remembers his wife, all abashed, with her head bent down, entering his house for the first time....He remembers his wedding night....his love making....and he recalls the first confinement of his wife....his becoming the father of three children within six years....The pitiful state of his mind when he finds out that his eldest son is a lunatic....And he is reminded of the ghastly fear about his second son....Who becomes shrewder and dishonest day by day....and of his dead third child: he remembers....a candid and beautiful girl resembling her mother....so many years have elapsed, but Antushet has not forgotten her face....he sights her always in the mind....as she was....ditto....

—ssuh|||—Antushet wakes up from his thoughts ....A snake drags itself in front of Autushet, treading upon the fallen dry leaves of trees....in the light of the lantern and moonlight, his eye follow the disappearing body of the snake....remain fixed in that direction....even after the disappearance, Antushet gazes for a long times as if hypontised....

★ ★ ★

"A snake, a snake...." he murmurs.... "Vinu is a snake....nothing can be judged of him....how he may get rid of his elder brother Mukund, cannot be known...." Antushet ponders.... "It is good that Parvati died....otherwise she would have certainly committed suicide after seeing her shrewd, heartless younger son Vinu...."

....And Antushet remembers his wife....always helpful....good manager....While she was alive, Antushet's gold profession was in prosperous condition....he recalls her sudden demise again and again....she who bore his children, she who was one with him....her face standing in front of his eyes as soon as he thinks of her....

....The muscle in the Antushet's neck moves....he stops for a deep breath....starts walking again....The circle of his thoughts revolves fast....Two years after the death of his wife, Antushet marries his halfmad son to a good-natured and hard-working girl....Mukund's wife behaves normally for the first two years....serving her father-in-law....in all respects, trying to help her husband....Antushet toils with new enthusiasm....begins to hoard some appreciable amount, but feels ill at ease at deteriorating character of Vinu....at his bad behaviour....

....And then Antushet gets cancer....Vinu finds all the freedom he wanted....now Antushet cannot keep Vinu under control by shouting at him....cannot oppose him....he has to keep quiet himself....Because he cannot speak due to cancer....

....Antushet has to note all the changes now....the madness of Mukund increasing....shrewdness of Vinu getting more aggressive....Vinu's evil net around Mukund's wife, he has to observe without any efforts to break it....he cannot protest against Mukund's vicious spell....

....Antushet has to keep quite....he has to observe the happenings as the....incidents of two days before....and just keep quiet.

....He had heard some noise in the rear of his house....taking his torch, he had entered the kitchen like a cat without producing a slightest sound....and he saw what he ought not to see....Vinu and Mukund's wife stood up swiftly....Antushet's sudden appearance had Mukund's wife dumb-founded....she even forgot to tidy her dishevelled clothes....Vinu fled away with his head down-cast....Antushet's eyes were expelling fire....so much shamelessness....so much immoral sex-hunger....the muscle in his neck was moving up and down.....its vibrations produced a peculiar sound....slowly had Mukund's wife moved past him with her face down-cast....as if hypnotised....And Antushet had seen....He had seen what he should not have seen....and he had no remedy over it....no solution....Because he was dumb....He could not speak....

"What sin makes me suffer this way?" Antushet questions himself.... "If I wanted....?"

He could have cheated the poor farmers like other goldsmiths....He could have sold the ornaments of copper-mixed gold....This way he could have erected a two-storey house like others....but never had Antushet thought of that way....he was humble....he was honest in his profession....

"Antushet is good old goldsmith." This qualifications offered to him by poor farmers had made him feel that we was going in a right way....He felt himself fit for that honest opinion....he had felt gratified....

"I might have sinned in the previous birth of mine...." Antushet answers himself...."when I die I shall find peace....I shall be free of this sin....I shall be given no more punishment....God almighty shall have pardoned me....I shall get eternal peace...."

And in that silver moonlight, Antushet hears the sounds of a distant church-bell....Tears roll down his eyes....With candid satisfaction that God had heard him....God had assured him....

Chapter XVI

THE HYPOCRITE
Datta Naik

ATMA's belly has met his back....From yesterday his old mother's health is deteriorating....The old woman continues her chattering and muttering though Death crawls towards her.... Except yesterday's stale kanji, Atma's belly is storing nothing....The kanji after staling his belly, stales his mind....In Atma's life nothing new, nothing fresh occurs....Every thing the same....stale....without any freshness....

Atma does not know his age....He remembers his mother taking him to the village landlord's house in his childhood at the time of festivals and other religious ceremonies....Now, at such times, he goes himself with *fatashi* (bamboo guns) and *pantle* (baskets)....to collect stale and tasteless remains of the feasts....to sell the bamboo guns and *teflan* to the sons of land-lords.

If somebody's cattle dies....and if Atma gets a chance he brings it to "Mharvado"....his body perspires out vesselful sweat to season its skin....He eats that dead, rotten stale flesh himself and receives the blessings of other "Mhars" for offering them some portion....The entrails of the dead animal are eaten by crows....The rotten flesh stinks.....This makes the landlords take their "dhoti" to their noses while passing by....Abusing and denouncing mothers and sisters of all other people, his old mother teaches him to stitch bamboo ribbon baskets and mats....His neighbour Pando gives him lessons as to how to beat the *dhol*....in front of the temple at the time of Diwali and other festivals....And hearing the abuses of the old hag, bearing *teflan* from bamboo guns, listening to Pandu's drum beats and smelling the stink of rotten and dead flesh, Atma's "atmaha" stales day by day....but still Atma grows....

★ ★ ★

"ATMA asare thain?" (Is Atma there?)

Atma's sleeping ears and eyes wake up....He sights the village doctor Giri Desai....Atma knows that during the Portuguese regime, Giribab was in prison for five years due to some "Jai Hind" affair....when "Jai Hind" came and the Portuguese went away, he turned himself into a leader....No ancestors from Atma's family have ever gone to the doctor....if the white-skinned children of village *Bamans* got diarrhoea, then his old mother goes to remove their curse by making yeast-dolls and frees them of the evil eye of the wicked....She afterwards brings the yeast-dolls evil eye home, roast them and satisfy their bellies....

"What is it, *batkar?* Any cattle dead?"

"Oh....we got no cattle at all to die....you know something, Atma? you know what is there to-day? your Sanjivayya is coming today...."

"Who is this Sanjivayya, *batkar*?"

"*Arre*, he is the President of the Congress Party who gave freedom to Goa....How is that you know nothing?"

The words "freedom", "Congress Party", "President" etc., are new to Atma....They reveal him no meaning....

"*Arre* Atma....He is from you Mhars,....This Mhar....sorry....this Harijan has become a great man by education....he is sitting besides Nehru....This great man comes to our place today....to see you....to see us....we must celebrate his coming....Now liberty dwells in Goa....this caste-systems should be abolished....I am a *Baman*....but look here, I am entering your hut...."

Up to now the old hag listens with rapt attention....when Giri Desai enters the hut, she tries to stand up dump-founded....and her sudden motion, makes her feel faint and she stumbles down again....Village Baman and he enters a Mhar's hut!!....The old hag pinches her withered body to see whether she is really awake or dreaming....

"*Age,* Atma's mother....don't get excited....Mhar....Baman are one....Nehru's right hand Sanjivayya is coming today....even you should come to welcome him...."

"The mother cannot walk....she is having fever from yesterday...."

"She is having fever and you are not letting me know? You come with me right now....I give you a prescription....you get the medicine from pharmacy."

The doctor tells Atma without caring to examine the old woman with stethoscope...."and do one thing Atma....please try to tell this Sanjivayya's coming to all Mahras....and after about one hour you come along with some four, five men....to welcome him, we are to decorate the roads with bamboo arches....All right then, I go ahead...."

Giri Desai goes away....Atma feels something new....something unusual circulates in him....and shortly the whole Mharvado knows that Nehru's favourite worker Sanjivayya is coming..... He takes all the bamboos that he had brought to make baskets, on his head and goes to town hurriedly....Hurriedly Giri Desai tells him the works...seeing him so busy, Atma does not dare to ask the prescription for old hag....He thinks of taking it afterwards and keeps quite....And in the hot sun, he works very hard....As the old hag is sick, he has not brought his meals with him.....he does not have even a Paisa in his pocket....Giri Desai is very busy....He oversees the work by shouting and moving here and there. So Atma cannot ask from him....Atma cannot even drink water....The hotel owners are not yet so progressed as Giribab....they still consider him untouchable and Atma has no guts to question them of his rights....

And Sanjivayya comes....seeing his black complexion, Atma agrees in his mind that he is a Mhar....Sanjivayya talks in some unknown language....A man interprets his speech in Konkani....and

The Hypocrite

Atma hears the same words of Giribab again...."freedom,", "Congress Party...."

From somewhere Giribab approaches Atma with a garland....He catches his hand with his....

"Atma, now you shall garland Sanjivayya...."

Atma's body shivers....He feels all this something new....something fresh....and like a cowherd leading his calf by its ear, Giri Desai leads Atma to rostrum....Atma garlands the President. Sanjivayya accepts in with a smile and *namaskar*....and Atma stands there stupidly....all nervous....

"Arre you should return the *namaskar*...."

Atma is all abashed....He falls on the ground with a humble *namaskar*....all people around giggle....Giribab makes him rise and sends him back....and after some time Giribab disappears with Sanjivayya....their car passing through the cheering crowd....

★ ★ ★

Atma strokes his hungry belly with his hand....the old hag prescription?....his daily wages? "Are, you are working for your person," This sentence of Giribab is his today's pay....

"Something new will happen....something fresh will happen...." Atma tries to make his mind believe that....but yesterday's stale kanji has staled his mind completely....Atma starts walking towards Maharvado with his weak legs and hungry stomach....

Chapter XVII

THE GREATEST SHOW ON EARTH
Abdul Majeed Khan

It was not for nothing that Hamid was careless about his leghorn these days. It was the most successful of all hens in that it had hatched all the twenty and the nascent chickens had become a nuisance so soon. They would rush into the kitchen and plunge into utensils containing food. They would imprint their dirty feet on clothes. They had proved themselves a menace to Hamid's beds of flowers and vegetables. The mother-hen had taught all the tricks to its young ones. So Hamid had to drive them off the fence.

The mother-hen was all eyes and would proudly cackle and sturt among the lucas plants, ceasal pinna and kikar bushes. But sadly the chickens were reduced to thirteen in two weeks. Each chicken had several lives as and when it was saved from the attack of the hawk and the mungoose. When they grew into young hens and cocks Hamid became somewhat negligent. He would have been content if only six were left. He had pinned his hopes on two white cocks one of which he called Rustom and the other Gama.

Now they had started quarrelling among themselves. The mother would watch from the shade of the lantana bushes. The fight would be mostly between Rustom and Gama. Others would gather round the mother and a few would show off themselves sitting on the back of the mother. Often there would be a tough fight for the coveted seat. They would display the same amount of jealousy and malice as politicians do in the election times.

The duelling pair would come into the sun and each leap with its beak ready to peck and pierce. They would dash forward, retreat, flourish their feathers and rush at each other with added venom. The other chickens watched as spectators around an arena, some sympathising with one and some with the other. Some would be satisfied by just imagining that they were themselves the fighters forgetting their existences and in hitting the imaginary opponent they would dab their mother's body with their beaks and she jumped up screaming: The bout between the two is disturbed. They become conscious of their mother's safety and give up their fight and make towards her.

Added to the older ones these fowls had multiplied Hamid's coops and his negligence followed suit. Now he nursed the notion that even if some of them had become a prey to the mungoose—for they were too big and strong to be victimised by hawks or crows—his loss would not be great. As if understanding this the fowls would run defiantly under the impression that the end of their life was just death either at Hamid's hands or in the maw of the mungoose. Peril or no peril was the same to them.

Once blistering afternoon the fowls were resting among the bushes helter shelter. But Rustom had gone very far and was reposing in a secluded bush. The cool shade of the green hedge was enough to inspire even a cock to go into a reverie. And as Rustom hid his beak in his feathers he was awakened to a sudden stir among the bushes. He became alert; a sudden fear shook him to his spine and he stood enthralled before a wild mungoose.

Now there was no time to escape. All his strength seemed to freeze. Before he could enjoy a little self-pity the mungoose leapt to seize him by the neck. But Heaven knows from where Rustom got his strength but he dodged aside and instead of his neck only a mouthful of his feathers fitted the mouth of the mungoose. He felt bitter pain as a volley of his tender feathers was plucked and blood drops dribbled slowly. He lost his voice. But a wave of heat ran through his flesh and in a desperate mood he rushed at his enemy and struck his beak straight into its face. The mungoose got the shock of his life for the first time and before he could spit out the lump of feathers Rustom ran round and inflicted injuries on his vile foe. His power of flight stood him in good stead. He attacked and fell on his enemy from all sides constantly changing his position. He gave the adversary no time to breathe!

Before all this could happen in a few fleeting second's tie he saw, as if by miracle, a big cobra slowly lowering its head directly over that of the mungoose. The latter was about to start at Rustom with all his venom and range when the cobra hissed at and stung pat pat on his neck. Now Rustom was puzzled and excited and a sense of courage at this god-sent ally made him crouch in a pose to attack his enemy.

The mungoose, now in a fix shifted his anger to his most natural enemy, and had furious bites at the body of the snake. He would have sliced the serpent into shreds but for Rustom's strategic interference. He grew more agile and gave the mungoose a tough time. When in the fraction of a second the mungoose would have bitten off the snake's head he lodged his beak straight into one eye of his enemy and then into the other.

What luck! The eyes of the mungoose began bleeding and he ran desperately for life. With a few gashes on his body and eyes torn he crept into the interior of the dark bushes. Rustom saw the cobra slowly creeping back into the bush.

His triumphant cackle remained unexpressed, before others of his kind, when he had to writhe in agony due to a sprinkling of some powder—Heaven knows what—at Hamid's hands. He was imprisoned for three days in his coop. The fourth day he came out crowing wildly.

More by instinct than by curiosity he went near the same spot where three days ago the battle had been waged. He saw his own silken feathers still scattered and strewn among dry leaves. The rustle of leaves due to a gush of wind startled him. And as he surveyed the dark grooves with an inhibited sense of dread he saw the serpent again coiling round a bulky branch. He thought the serpent frequented the spot and with a fearful curiosity fixed his gaze on the dreaded reptile. But there was no sign of a stir or a hiss. And his unsteady legs carried him very near the trysting serpent. He wanted to convey him gratitude to the snake and clucked co-co-rico in his weakest tone.

The snake didn't pay any heed. And with the confidence that even if his goodwill was mistaken and the snake intended any harm he could run for life, he went closer to the snake and gently touched him with his beak. The snake dropped down his head at this as if ready to sting. But soon Rustom found that his fear was baseless, for the snake remained insert as a rope. He saw that the snake was cold stone-dead.

He was bewildered for a minute, a mixed feeling gripped his heart. He felt so sorry that he couldn't express his gratitude and started running back as fast as he could to tell the whole world his unique experience.

Chapter XVIII

ON THE FEAST OF SAN JOAO
Adelaide de Souza

THE Goa-bound bus trundled once again to an abrupt stop—the sixth in the last twenty five miles. And while the driver and his assistant tinkered with the engine, the grumbling passengers got off to stretch their cramped limbs. It was late evening and Francis doubted whether any transport would be available to take him to his own village Revora even if their Luxury Coach did reach the Mapuca township before dusk. The breakdown took place at a crossroad near Tivim, from which point a brisk stroll across the hills would take him to his home in less than an hour. He knew the route well. It brought back nostalgic memories of his school days. Where, he could go via Fortir and if his cousin Clare's folk were at home, he could have a "shakedown" there for the night and go to Revora the next morning. The more he thought of it, the more the idea appealed to him. It was years since he had visited his relatives at Fortir and the frightening appeal of that ghostly deserted little village held more fascination for him than any other village in Goa.

The driver hailed a passing taxi and the conductor was sent to Mapuca for some spares. That decided Francis collecting his small case he got off the bus.

Francis looked around him—his heart bursting with pride and pleasure. This was his home—the Goa he loved. It was well worth the long and tiring journey by bus, a fitting reward for the eleven months of cramped never-ceasing grinding his life in the crowded Metropolis was. This one month of rest and peace in his own hometown!

He was glad now that circumstances had made it impossible for him to take his leave in the month of May as he had hoped. True, most of the fruit the cashews, jackfruit and mangoes were off-season now. And so were the weddings and the 'festas'. But with the first rains everything was lush and green and peaceful. He breathed in large gulps of fresh air and whistled gaily as he trod along.

In the distance he heard the sound of beating drums and as he passed the creek he saw the "sangodd" and remembered. Today was "San Joao"—the feast of St. John the Baptist celebrated perhaps with more zest than all the other local feasts. So the festivals were by no means over. He had participated in this celebrations only once—just after he had finished school. He recalled the gaiety and thrill of it all. The old and the young as frolicsome as children as they plunged into wells to the cheers of the admiring spectators. The singing and the toasts when they went round the village collecting "aliso". He wished he had come a day earlier but he had forgotten all about "San Joao". He would have loved to have been in it, he thought.

But he was soon in it. For at the end of the lane, he met a gay party of young men wearing coronets of flowers, their bodies glistening wet after their plunge in the well. Among them, was his co-villager Joaquim who had married a girl from his side of Tivim. As is the custom, the sons-in-law are guests at their wives' home for this feast and Joaquim insisted that Francis join them. Francis agreed to having a drink. One drink led to another and it was dusk before Francis left the party despite the very pressing invitation of his hosts to spend the night with them. He would spend the night at Fortir, which was only a short distance away, he told them, for he had learnt from Joaquim that his Aunt was at home.

It wasn't dark when he started out. But it was darkening. Night comes on so eerily on the moors and hill-sides. Francis was not a fanciful creature so he didn't mind that. But he did mind choosing the wrong path in the dusk and having to walk back miles. And he did choose the wrong path. These short cuts, he cursed, are the longest possible tracks from somewhere to somewhere via nowhere or it may have been the caju feni.

As it grew darker Francis began to wonder whether he shouldn't walk back and accept Joaquim's hospitality after all. He wished he had at least borrowed a light. He would ask for a candle or better still a 'Goa torch' made of palm leaves that gave better light than a three cell torch, at the very next homestead he saw. From the moat came the dark smell of water-weeds and the faint smell of wild jasmine—and Francis knew he had nearly reached his destination at Fortir.

Suddenly the leaves of the trees began to quiver with increased urgency. Was it going to rain? A sudden quiet fell. Even the sound of the leaves faltered to a trembling murmur. The notes of the birds became fainter, fugitive and evanescent, until they too ceased and there was silence—complete frightening silence. Francis looked around desperately and saw the only house in that vicinity.

The house seemed deserted. It was filthy and derelict. But one thing made him stare and stare. At the open window, with light of the bottle—lamp shining full on her, stood a woman, her hair flowing down on her shoulders, a garland of jasmines wound like a coronet on her head. He stood by the bush debating whether he should ask a light from this strange woman when she called out to him. "Come in Francisco—don't be afraid little one!"

It was then he remembered her. It was "Mad Juana" of course. She lived alone on the top of the hillock a few hundred yards from his Aunt's house. He was now surer of his bearings.

On the Feast on San Joao

He recalled his first encounter with Juana. While visiting his Aunt, (he must have been about ten years old at the time) he had trespassed into Juana's compound in search of squirrels, when she had hailed him just as she did now and after feeding him with mangoes, had presented him with two squirrels which she trapped with the greatest ease. Animals were not afraid of her nor she of them. He had heard a story of how she fed a cobra, with milk and was actually seen beating it with a little stick when it didn't obey her. She was passionately fond of children too and there were always sweets for those who called to see her.

Juana had lost her only child at birth and her husband, a sailor, had died at sea. That was when Juana had gone "crackers", and though she was normal in every other way, she still clung to the belief that her husband would one day return. In fact, she wrote herself imaginary letters which she insisted came from her husband.

Francis wondered how Juana could have recognized him after so many years and in the dark too. Well! mad people had a sixth sense he had heard. Perhaps that accounted for it. He hesitated no longer but made his way up the steps and found the door open. There was naught in the room save two old rickety chairs, an old chest and a large dining table. The air smelt musty as though it had not seen the light of the sun for years. But on the table was a tray laden with fruit. A large slice of jackfruit, bananas and luscious rosy mangoes seen only in Goa in this season. There were also some sannas and worde which reminded Francis that he was hungry. It's my "aliso" she explained "but the boys haven't come to collect it yet. It is an offering to celebrate my baby's birth and my husband's home coming. You didn't know he had come home?" she asked seeing the look of surprise on my face. "He has," she continued, "as I always knew he would. He has gone with the others to celebrate "San Joao".He should be back any moment now". There was a wild look in her eyes. Poor Juana, thought Francis, she seems much worse mentally at least. For only then did it strike him that she looked younger and more beautiful than he remembered her. He asked her if he could borrow a light—for he was now very anxious to leave. "But you can't leave now", Juana said determinedly "Why it's raining and I'm terrified of storms. You can't leave—you can't. My husband will soon be here. See there he is!" she exclaimed pointing through the open window. There was a loud clap of thunder and a flash of lightening so bright that it let up the whole country-side. On the edge of the well, poised like a diver and looking like a Greek God stood a man. "There he is! That's him!" screamed Juana. "It's my husband! He mustn't! He'll never come back! Let me go to him!" And before he knew what was happening, she had pushed Francis aside and had run out into the night. He heard a splash and ran in the direction she had gone—it was to the well at the edge of the compound. The next flash of lightening showed her floating in the water, her upturned face begging or help—arms waving wildly. The well had no protecting wall nor was there any rope nearby. Francis stripped off his shirt. Perhaps if he tore it up it would serve. Suddenly he found himself being dragged into the well. He felt himself slipping—slipping—slipping.

When he came to, he found himself at his Aunt's house. A doctor was standing at the foot of his bed watching him. Francis remembered everything. But here was a great deal he still wanted to know. The doctor listened intently as Francis talked and what he said when Francis had his say, angered the young man so much that he sprang out of his bed. It was only the heavy weight of his plastered foot that kept him pinned there.

"Oh no doctor", he said heatedly, "I'm not the victim of any hallucination. Nor was I drunk last night. I am naturally anxious to know what happened to poor Juana and her husband." In his heart he felt he knew what had happened to them. "I was too late, wasn't I? They were both drowned weren't they?"

The doctor looked at his Aunt. Then he seemed to make up his mind. He said "Juana was drowned in the well yes." "and her husband?" asked Francis "Drowned at sea twenty years ago" was the reply.

"But I saw him. Juana claimed it was her husband—just before she followed him and killed herself". Francis insisted. His Aunt smiled pityingly at him while she explained:

"Juana was drowned when she jumped in the well on the feast of San Joao five years ago. The well has been dry and unused ever since. That's the well you fell into in the dark."

Chapter XIX

A TALE WITHOUT WORDS
Rui Peres

I HAD always thought of writing a story, a story that was real, like Life, perhaps, more real than Life. When I was barely five (how long ago that seems now!) I urged to tell my father:

"Father, you invent stories about wolves and jackals. Why don't you tell me something that really happened?.... Something about you."

But I was scared. Father was imposing and hot-tempered and mad when angry. Even whilst relating the anecdote about the tiger and the lamb, he would raise his voice so loud, that mother had often to scurry from the kitchen with her hands smeared from kneading chapaties to see what was wrong. But she would sprint back to her work as if nothing had disturbed her. She cowered before him. One day when he did request father to lower his voice, he spurted forth such a roar that it sounded like a bursting cracker and mother turned pallid. Father was not the sort of man you could talk to at night.

His chest bulged with muscles; his arms were as strong as the branches of a mango tree; only they were dark with the sun. Moreover, as he never wore a shirt except on Sundays when he went for Mass, anybody could be instilled with fear at the sight of them.

During the day he toiled in the landloard's fields and every evening he brought some money home which he gave to mother after setting aside a few coins for himself. Mother, too, was out for the better part of the day as she went daily to the master's house in order to draw water, and wash clothes. At ten in the morning she would cook the rice, prepare fish-curry and carry along with her a portion of the food.

When they returned at sunset they were both tired. 'Mai' was usually back by six-thirty chewing tobacco which she stored inside the furrow of her gaudy folds and whenever she extracted a fresh particle it appeared she was deliberately loosening her baggy wraps in order to display her navel. Her teeth were becoming brown due to the leaves she consumed but father never said anything to her. Probably because he knew when to leave her alone and when to say what, that is, so long as she didn't disturb his evening moods; he was too jolly to notice the little kinks in her character.

Carrying me in his arms he then sang and told me stories about wolves and jackals preying on weaker creatures, and how they always killed but were seldom killed themselves. There was not a day he did not swear. Very often he uttered words that I could not comprehend; they were bad words, I learned later. He swore them so naturally that they seemed as innocent as the lambs and rabbits, as profuse as the copper bangles that jingled on mother's arms and as meaningless, besides.

★ ★ ★

Ours was a simple way of life, without dates, and so uneventful that it is difficult to remember incidents except in terms of unorganised pictures as the years rolled by.

One day mother had no money for rice. Father had been kicked from the landlord's house for back-answering his wife. He came straight home and went to sleep. He was drunk. Without an anna in his pocket, and today, Mai was saying, was Saturday, that means, an empty stomach tomorrow.

Mother was worried. I thought and thought and suddenly I hit upon a novel idea. "Mother, why don't you sell one of your bangles? You have so many."

She smiled with irritation: "Are you out of your mind?"— I was preparing for Holy Communion then, nearing the age of eight, and consequently was expected to have some sense.

That evening mother went to the landloard's house to beg for his forgiveness. He was kind enough to give her a measure of rice and a rupees, but asked her to return the next day in order to mop the "sala" and clean the house as his daughter's birthday was approaching.

She came home happy and sermonised that Anton had to change his ways, or else he would he cursed by God and men. I could not but agree, for father had lately increased his consumption of spirits.

Luckily, father wasn't eavesdropping, or he might have landed me a blow on the head or a slap. I was no longer his pet now. Three more children had adorned our home. The days of stories were over; instead I had to look after my brothers and sisters, and work during the day; helping mother with her cooking in the morning, and whenever father fell senseless on the streets, or came home fuzzled I was expected to chafe salt against his hands and feet, and ignore the bad words he unwittingly railed at me.

★ ★ ★

The 3rd of December feast of St. Francis Xavier is a great day in Goa....That morning I was decked in a crumpled white frock with long sleeves (the first time I wore a frock) and prepared myself to receive God. As I knelt before the communion rails what struck me was my awkwardness compared to the graceful gestures of the other girls in white. They were younger than me but so primly dressed! Their frocks shone white like the veil of the Virgin, and every movement of their feet seemed to remind me of dolls, the kind of expensive dolls I once saw displayed at a fair. One of them was pink in complexion, brown-eyed and had long hair falling in cascades behind her ears, which were delicate as wax-petals. She had a flowered ribbon on her head decorated with white trinkets.

After Mass father, who wore a clean red shirt and a brown pant, pulled me by the hand. He was taking me home, but mother said: "Wait, I want to take her to "bai's" house."

"For what?" Father was usually quick tempered in the mornings. But he permitted.

She lived in a big house cemented from the entrance to the passage which led to the back-door, and its ceiling rested so high that it could easily engulf four huts one on top of the other and hardly fill a room. How tiny our hut seemed compared to this mansion!

Mother led me inside holding hard my right hand as if she feared I might be lost in those tunnel-like, winding corridors. A lady met us on the way. She was tall and fair, and though she looked old she wore a gold brooch and an elegant maroon dress. She smiled affably, adding: "Is this the mischief-maker?" Mother mumbled blushing; the colour of the red trinkets in her necklace was reflected on her face, while I stood mute, not knowing what to say, but at the same time experiencing a sense of tingling elation in her remark.

While I was thus engrossed I suddenly noticed in the lady's face an approaching cloud of apprehension. "Look out" she shrieked staring beyond me, "The dog." But there was no time. Before I could grasp the dark significance of her words, I felt my wrist being violently grabbed and shaken. Oh, what pain! I screamed falling back like a log. A huge black dog was over me, its bulging eyes emitting sparks of fury. There was a commotion; mother was wailing; I thought I must die. In my agony the saving words. "Mother" "God" "Virgin" which I learnt from mother and in the catechism classes dragged themselves out of my mouth.

Evidently Christ heard my piercing lamentations: Somebody came rushing towards me, kicked the dog and pulled it by the tail. I was free, thank God, but ivied watching my own blood on my palm and fingers dribbling like slaver out of an old man's mouth. Only his was red and dark.

A slim girl bright-eyed and genial washed my lacerations and administered tincture. She was the landlord's daughter. I divined it the moment she observed casting a glance over my dress, "Wasn't this my frock, Mummy?" The elderly lady nodded her head benevolently, whilst suddenly reminding herself that she would be late for Mass if she delayed any more. In a second she was gone admonishing behind her back: "Give them coffee and bread, Clara, will you?"

For the first time in my life I tasted butter; perhaps the last too. Because father was a poor man and like most poor men unreasonably concluded that all who ate butter became fat and dozed on arm-chairs. Take, for instance, the landlord. Is he not a walking barrel, and what work does he do?

Father had a grudge against the landlord. Under the slightest pretext he would invoke his name in order to explain his points and prove his generations. Oftentimes the latter were so absurd that the landlord himself would have laughed at hearing them.

★ ★ ★

But all that seems such a long time ago as I now think of it. Years have flown by swifter than pigeons. The bird of time has clipped a new badge on my breast. I am no longer a maid.

It happened in a flash. Mother announced one day that I would have to outgrow my childish ways to be a good mother; that I would have to teach my husband how to live in accordance with God's Commandments.

I recollect that Sunday with a blush; when decked in a long

white cloth wound around my body in luxuriant folds, I was escorted to the church, and how I hid my face because I was too shy to show it to my relatives, lest they might smile and crack silly jokes about me.

My husband was a healthy brown in complexion, young and string; within less than a year he gave me a son, who is sprouting like a tender shoot. Someday, when little Francis grows up and comes out of School with a diploma in hand, and calls me to live with him, then, perhaps, we may live in a big house and taste butter everyday and remember that great day twinkling amidst the bleached left-overs of the Past, the day I wore a white frock and went for First Holy Communion and taste Creamery in the Landlord's house with my frock soiled and my hand still bloody from the bite.

I have hopes. So many of our children are now going to school. Newer and newer pigeons are coming and going, bringing with them the latest chippings of new hopes. But I wonder....the future is not, I think, like the past through which we can see clearly. Times are changing. Invisible to the pigeons are the dark clouds roving over our heads after each sunset. Every day somebody is lost in the wake of the approaching darkness, and a familiar face disappears without leaving behind a trace. Where is the landlord today and that tall lady who wore a gold brooch? and where is my father who once used to tell me stories? Who knows, a day might come when we'll have to forget the folk lore and start telling something about ourselves, of labour, hardships, liquor and peace. After all, are not our experiences also good enough to be clothed in stories?

That was why I had thought of reminding father to tell me a real story, although in that distant past, I never knew I would be following his footsteps. Destiny is so ironical!....Yes, every night Francis listens attentively, while I conceal myself behind my baggy folds. So I ever tell him about the tortures I underwent attending on father every night, my heart cracking with each gasp he uttered from the ulcer in his stomach and about mother not knowing what to do because there was no money to pay the doctor; reassuring her self that it was merely a stomach-ache he had, a trivial illness. All she did, I thought then, was to chew tobacco and slur her teeth. But what else could she do? Did she have a hundred rupees to take father to Bombay or buy the quires of prescriptions the doctors would recommend?

Nobody knew, anyway, that father's hour was drawing to a close until one day she decided to call in our village doctor. He was a short gentleman, old bulky, burdened with a pot-like paunch and showing a depressed face behind his thick glasses. He examined the emaciated body on the mat, washed his hands, and then when mother accompanied him to the door with a crumpled note in her hand, he remarked sullenly "It's a pity. You dullards always wait till the last moment." He refused to accept the money; and, what moved me and mother deeply, was his sudden gesture, like and avalanche of tenderness "Take this" he said flicking out two ten-rupees notes from his pocket "Give him whatever he wants. It's the end."

That night I wept; realizing that the world was not as bad as it seemed. There were some men, some angels sent by God; to relieve suffering. A few they were, but they were worth the name.

Year later, when the doctor died and I attended his funeral contrary to the prevailing custom, I could see the black flap of his coffin being weighed down with every spadeful of the murky earth, just as it had done over the concealed form of my father, so many, many, years ago. And I thought then how vain it was to live and be rich, and I prayed for his soul with eyes moist with memories. One day I too would be like them: a lump of hard clay whom only the grave embraces and claims as her children.

But who will write about this, the sad truth concerning man's life and ours, poor as we are? Perhaps, Francis, someday, divining my thoughts will take the burden upon himself and write a real story, the story about the Lilliputians of the earth.

Like a hopeful mother I pin my faith in him, leaving the rest to God.

Chapter XX

THE PICKPOCKET
Filbert Pires

RAJANI was watching the football game with much enthusiasm even though he had not purchased the entrance ticket. Not that he did not have the 50 paisa for the ticket—he had received his pay of Rs. 120/- just today—but then would have to account it to his wife. And if his wife only came to know that he had spent the sum of 50 paisa on a football ticket; well, you could hardly describe the scene that would follow.

"You idiot, wasting money to see some stupid fools chasing a ball. What do you think I should do, see the prices...wheat at 60 paisa a kilo, no petrol in the house, and what would you do if we had children?"

As these thoughts were crossing his mind, a lonely hand was fumbling with the button of his hind pocket.

"Ah!" rose a murmur from the crowd—the ball had struck the goal-post and had rebounded for another kick. It was surely going in now. The excited crowd kick. It was surely going in now. The excited crowd was on edge, and Rajani was rising to his toes.

"Go—a—l" followed by clapping, it was a clean shot. This goal would finish the First Division Games of the Season. only a minute left for the end.

"Hello Rajani," it was his friend Baptist from the Office, "enjoying the game, hem?"

Rajani blushed, which was usual with him, "Well, a very exciting game; did you see this goal now?" asked Rajani.

The Pickpocket

"Damn the goal" said Baptist, "had it not been for it, I would still have 50 bucks in my pocket. I just lost a bet."

"Well...." began Rajani.

"What well, come on let's go," said Baptist, "the game is over now. What about a drink?"

"I....er" began Rajani, "you know today is payday, I have got to go home early my wife will be anxiously waiting for me". With this he touched his hind pocket with a smile. "Ah!....What! my purse," he murmured. "Why, my purse has been snatched." His face turned purple, and he was fumbling in all his pockets now, but in vain. The football game was over by now, and the rushing crowd forced them out.

"I told you," began Baptist, "specially at these games; all who come are not football fans, you should be careful". They walked quietly down the road, Rajani's thoughts rushing through his mind. "What would his wife say; surely, she would not believe that his purse was stolen."

"All right then boy, coming with me, I am going to the 'Sol-Mar'" said Baptist.

"No, no I am going home" said Rajani.

They separated and Rajani made his way to the 'Jardin' to think over. He had to fabricate something to account for the money. "My God" he thought, as he sat down on a bench, trying to invent something for his wife. "What a mess these pickpockets can make."

After some time he came to a decision. He could say that he had paid the grocery bills, the milkman and the rent as well, on his way home. This would amount Rs. 112/- The other eight? Er....he had reserved two tickets for 'Sangam'. She was keen fan of Raj Kapoor, and would definitely not bother more.

With a bright smile he got up. "Oh!", he screwed his eyebrows, but the milkman would come tomorrow morning with the milk, and he would ask for money.

"Damn it,' he murmured angrily, as his whole plan collapsed.

He sat for some moments, meditating.

"Yes, ... yes, the Banks were closed."

"Here it was, he could say the Banks were closed, and all payments were postponed until Monday, and then—well, he must somehow arrange the money on Monday." With this bright plan in his mind, he rose from his seat, and made his way through the 'Jardin'. He looked at his watch, "My God, it is 8.30". He began to walk hurriedly, when at the corner under a big banyan tree a man rolled drunkenly on the ground. Rajani looked at the drunkard in the darkness, who was obviously beyond this world. He shook him by the shoulders, "Hey, come on boy,—get up." As he rolled him, something slipped from the drunkards pocket. Rajani looked, it was the drunkard's wallet. Visions began forming in his mind, and he was perspiring. He picked the wallet up quietly, and opened it. Plenty of notes inside. He quickly dumped them in his pockets, looked at the drunkard snoring softly, and hurried from the spot.

He went to the side street, and made his way home.

"Where have you been Rajani" was his wife's greeting.

"Er....I was delayed at the Office," said Rajani, "you know today is Saturday. The boss kept me for some extra work."

"What about your pay?"

"Of course here it is" he replied, handing the crumpled notes to his wife. She counted them carefully, "A hundred, why a hundred a fifty six here, Rajani."

"Oh, the extra was last month's overtime" he said with as much glibness though he was perspiring.

"What a darling you are Rajani, you should always work extra; you know we need the money for...."

Rajani blushed, but inwardly his heart was coming to his throat. He walked quickly to their bedroom, removed his clothes, and went for a shower, thankful for the cold water to lighten his thoughts. "Bless the devil under the banyan tree" he muttered.

The Pickpocket

On Monday morning, Rajani with a light gaiety and with two tickets reserved for 'Sangam' in his pocket made his way to the Office, whistling softly.

"You look so happy today". It was Baptist.

"What to tell you," began Rajani, "when I left you yesterday evening—God bless the devil....What do you think happened?"

"Now wait a minute" said Baptist, "listen to me."

"Ahah."

"Your purse was pinched last evening, well my purse was pinched last night" exclaimed Baptist angrily.

"What...."

"See when I left you yesterday evening, I went to the 'Sol-Mar', ha a couple of drinks and when I was coming out whom do you think I met? Leela....Leela the typist. She came for a Coke. You know her talk, this and that. By this time she had 3 Cokes and I had belted six rums. I don't know when exactly she left me, but I remember I came to the 'Jardin' in the hope of finding you there. I must have passed out on the bench, for I found myself under the banyan tree in the morning—minus my purse."

"Hem...." muttered Rajani, he was feeling uneasy, and was perspiring profusely.

"You look so pale and worried" said Baptist.

"Er....I had thought of asking you a loan today," he blurted out at last.

Chapter XXI

THE RENUNCIATION
Rui Peres

"For what is your life? It is even a vapour, that appeareth for a little time, and then vanisheth away."

N. T., James, IV, 14

SERLA was the only thing she had or could ever hope to have from life. A little angel of four. That was her girl—her 'sherry' daughter brought into this world of bitterness through no fault of her own. Yet, she was destined to suffer—most crushingly—not the lethal blows of the physique, which are far lighter than mental, but the tortures of her thinking mind.

"Mummy, what are you thinking?" asked Serla with that innocent look of hers.

"Nothing, my Serla! Nothing!" she sighed; saying to herself within that vast reservoir where all her thoughts were stored, one superseding the other as the situation warranted, "Poor thing! She's too little to know". Then, all of a sudden, something—a newly refreshed idea—fluttered, and its fluttering sounds could be witnessed in the visible tracings of a broad smile. "Nothing my love. I was just thinking of the story I should tell you to-night in bed."

Serla smiled childishly and giggled with joy. She was very fond of hearing stories where fairies were concerned—how they loved in their world and never died. She liked to hear her mother say every night at the end of the story. "And they lived happily everafter." But her mother would now-a-days end the story, with:

"And that was the end of it all" or "And so it ends", or "they end," according to the number of fairies and princes and princesses taking part in the tale. And Serla would, sometimes, ask anxiously "But mummy, is the story over? You did not say that they lived happily and all that...."

"Yes, my child. The fairies die every night."

And then, when Serla's face would record gloom, her mother would say quickly, "My child, Why are you sad?—Because they die?"

"Yes. They shouldn't die!" She would reply.

"They shouldn't; but they die." And then, the mother would try to argue after the innocent ways of a child: "Your name is Serla. How can I call you 'Lisette'?"

"But you call me 'love,' 'Sherry;' 'my child' and so many things!"

This simplicity would evoke hearty laughters in the mother who would then bestow fond kisses on her flowery little angel. "Sleep, my child" she would say. "Forget the world...." Indeed! What a blessing it was to have this cherub near her bosom!

★ ★ ★

"Mummy, are you still thinking? I know now! You're thinking about this morning, when you took me to the church to hear the Sunday Mass...."

"Why....what happened this morning, my little one?" Luzia asked, trying to hide the concern in her face.

"Didn't you see?....While you were hearing the Pe. Vigario giving sermon from the pulpit, Aunt Livia pointed you out to her sister, who has come from Panjim to spend a few days with her...."

"She isn't your aunt, my child," her mother corrected, "she is just our neighbour. Anyway, what did she say?" Luzia couldn't help disguising her apprehensions.

"She pointed to you" Serla resumed "and whispered to her sister saying 'there's the Regedor's wife—I mean ex-Regedor who's become a leper....' And then her sister whispered back aloud, her face full of horror,—like the picture, mummy, of the devil you were showing me yesterday. She exclaimed 'the leper's wife! Oh God!....And who's the smiling little tot by her side,' I smiled" continued Serla innocently, unaware of the silent tears flowing down Luzia's face "I smiled, mummy. And then, suddenly, Aunt Livia,—no, our neighbour Livia said something to her sister again....Her sister scowled at me, and made an ugly face, like when I do when I take castor oil."

Luzia dared not make her stop. Her back turned upon the bed where her daughter lay, she looked at the dark sky outside the window. It seemed so dark, despite the numberless stars flickering upon its face; and although there was moon, it was but an almost wholly concealed 'D', emitting a dim glow over the distant Calangute beach. And the far away splashing of the waves, sometimes translating itself into an occasional roar, and the almost inaudible 'Serenada' and faint guitar much coming on from the gay merrymaking boys singing on the beach, seemed but a strange accompaniment to the innocent voice of the little angel relating the incident at the church, and the darkness outside another concomitant of it. "Yea, nature often joins in one's sorrows!" She thought.

"Mummy" she could hear her little Sherry say in that meek and guiltless voice of a child "Why do people make ugly faces at us? Why do they call you 'Leper's wife' and me his daughter?"

"Shut up!" Luzia screamed turning back, and then when she saw the startled look of her little Serla, she embraced her passionately, and flooded her smooth innocent face with kisses.

"My lovely Serla" she said "You must sleep now. It is ten....First say your prayers, my child."

"But mummy? What about the story?"

"O.K. I'll tell it afterwards" the prayers said, the small offering was made as usual. It consisted in lighting and adding more oil to the oil-lamp, and covering it up by a red container, open at the top, and then placing it before the big frame of Scared Heart of Jesus. And a final prayer for the deliverance from sin said aloud by both.

"What is sin? Is it a big cruel giant ready to eat every one up, or is it the evil deeds of the Bad Fairy?"

"No, my child. It is both. It is damnation on earth and deliverance in Heaven."

"I don't want to be damned, mummy! I want to be delivered like my dead father."

Luzia smiled sadly; controlling what was rising to her throat. "Poor little cherub!" she thought "She's still a raw fruit. How can she know the ravages of tempest? How can she know that the root that is hollow is supposed to be dead? How can she know the secrets that are concealed in each of the crevices, until the final showdown when they shall all be scattered by the winds and revealed? And what immediately will follow but a stark acknowledgement of FACT! Perhaps, the jolt may be felt, too hard—too startling for the existent sober normality. Indeed! It is the falling tree that has to bear the strains of concealment—not the tiny little leaves or branches, that are allowed to flap for the present without the fear of suspense. Anyway, won't the shock thereupon be shattering for those that never expected the tree to fall?....Suspense, perhaps, is better, because it prepares....it leads to expectancy, it makes one see as probably existent' what was thought 'not to be'. But, Luzia thought and here her spirit revolted against herself. How can I have the courage to tell her that her father is alive—that he is rotting away in that hospital at Macasana; waiting for death to have some mercy on him, by freeing him from the chains of that dreadful sort of death! How can I tell my little Serla that her father is damned forever from the society of men—that we are quarantined by the pangs of segregation for the rest of our lives—that she, my little lily of innocence....Just a few days back I heard my neighbour Estefira order her child not to play with Serla, not even to talk to her....Brutish, isn't it! To say this in front of my own child! Yet, I don't blame her. Wouldn't I have done the same were my own child concerned? It is hard, but we must live according to the vicissitudes of time! Certainly we must....

"Mummy" her daughter interrupted "is there a ghost on that dark coconut tree outside?"

"Why, my child?"

Because I saw you looking at it just now. Your face seemed so sad and serious, that I was frightened. I even forgot that you promised to tell me a story after I'd said my prayers. You'll tell me now, wont you mummy."

"Well," Luzia hesitated, "I shall tell you a nice story, a real one. Do you want to hear?"

"Yes, yes" Serla repeated with joy "Is it about fairies and princesses?"

"You will know...." she said. And presently, in a feverish manner she started in the usual way children love to hear a story:-

"Once upon a time there was a beautiful valley. In it lived a prince. He was tall, strong, and though a little dark, he was handsome. Everyone liked him because he was intelligent. Yes, he was very important in the valley. And all came to him to get their papers signed or to seek advice.

"This prince sometimes went to distant lands to carry out some of his work. On one of these occasions he saw a lonely princess, who had neither father nor mother...."

"Mummy, mummy," Serla cut in anxiously, "was the princes lovely?"

"I guess so," Luzia replied with a smile, "otherwise the prince wouldn't have fallen in love with her."

"Afterwards what, mummy? A Bad Fairy did her harm?"

"No, my child, not then but afterwards—they both got married and were very happy for a long time. They were especially overjoyed because a beautiful princess was born to them—much lovelier than her mother. But a dark fairy who was peeping into their house one day, was filled with jealousy, because she didn't like to see anyone happy. This fairy had a powerful spell—that whoever she spoke to would have a swollen face....and his body would rot. And this spell would again be transmitted to anyone that touched him. In this way, everyone would be forced to flee from him."

"Mummy was the fairy so bad?"

"Yes, my child. So one day she spoke to the prince."

"And then mummy....did no one stop the Bad Fairy? Didn't anyone warn the prince not to speak to the Bad Fairy?"

"No, my innocent angel. Thus one dark night when the Prince was sleeping with his wife and child, the Fairy came and touched the left hand of the prince..... The next morning, when he woke up, he was driven away—far away to a ravine; and his wife and child left...."

"But mummy, it wasn't his fault" the child protested.

"Yes, but everyone thought he was to blame. You see, Serla, that was the spell."

"I understand now," she said lowly, pretending she'd really understood "and I pity the princess and her lovely little daughter. Poor things! How bitterly they must have cried!"

Luzia's voice hardened "Yes, they wept, and those tears evaporated bringing down nothing....Every servant in the house refused to stay, and so the lonely ones had to live alone, doing as much they could of little money the Prince had kept behind for them. You know, Serla, even all those that had once been so friendly to the Prince and his wife, during the time of 'butter and cheese' never again entered the house, because the spell had a greater strength on them than gratitude—Even the relatives....just think of that! And it is fortunate that the house they lived in belonged to them; otherwise they'd have been driven out."

"Mummy, this story is very sad!" Serla lamented, "I don't want to hear it, mummy. But tell me....Did the princess never go to see her husband?"

"Why, my Serla, she went just once. She took her two years old daughter with her....this was one-and-a-half-year after the Prince had been sent to the Ravine. And there they met....

"The face of the Prince was all swollen up and his right eye was red, and his whole face had a redish kind of complexion—(colour, my child, due to the spell). And he looked sad and dreadful. But when he saw his wife coming; bringing the little one with her, he laughed aloud with sorrow and wept soon afterwards. 'Is this my little apple?' he said jokingly. Yet his face looked so sad, frightful that nothing coming from those swollen lips could seem like a joke. 'Oh God!' he exclaimed suddenly 'why have I disgraced the little apple? Why have I disgraced you?"

"And then the princess reminded him that it wasn't his fault—that it was due to the spell set forth by the Bad Fairy. But he only kept staring at the child, or its mother weeping now and then, aloud from the place which separated him from his dear ones—outside the wire wall. Finally, he said 'Good-bye' in a touching voice. And when he saw his wife trying to come closer, he said "No, don't come nearer." And he poured flying kisses on both of them; and seeing the little child stare at him, as if trying to recollect something that was long over, he said affectionately 'God bless you, my little doll'. And sobbing, he ran inside and joined the others, who were also under the same spell."

"Mummy," Serla said suddenly "wasn't there any good fairy to make him well again? There should be a good person among

The Renunciation

the bad, isn't it mummy? You've always said that in your stories...."

"No, my child. In really life there are only bad fairies—those that live to do evil, and like to do it."

The child heard her mother with a blank face. She was a lily yet. "Good night, mummy" she prattled.

★ ★ ★

Luzia kissed her daughter good-night—She had just closed her eyes and was treading down the smooth depths of the valley where innocence found its sleep. Nevertheless when she felt the warmth of her mother's lips on her cheeks, she opened her little brown eyes unsteadily and smiled, extending her delicate hands and holding her mother's neck so as to return the kiss on the natural red of her lips. But the long dark hair her mother had fell profusely on her olive face and eyes, making everything seem black. She kissed the hair, and immediately afterwards let her head fall back on the soft pillow again.

The mother blew off the candle, which was stuck on to a metal stand on the table, beside the bed....A dim red of the lamp was the only light in the room. There was no electricity.

She returned to the window....the distant swashing of the waves and the occasional roar continued. The music of the guitars could be heard more audibly. she strained her ears and could distinguish faintly the soft notes of the song "Tudo acabou, tudo morreu" (All is over, nothing is left) which was being sung. Oh yes! Today was the 30th of April—the last day of the month for many busy holiday-goers, who didn't intend visiting the Calangute beach, until the April of next year....As she tried to hear, she could see the indistinct outlines of the many coconut trees, standing tall of the soft sands o the beach. And then suddenly she heard the muffled thud of a falling coconut. The unexpected sound startled her and she felt afraid of something she knew not....It was believed through out the village that a coconut falling out at night meant the coming of some disaster to anyone who heard it.

★ ★ ★

Luzia closed the window, applied the latch to its protecting door and returned to the bed where she slept with her daughter. It was a double bed, the same bed where she used to sleep with her husband....What joys had they shared during those days in each other's company!....but what was the use of lingering now over those faded, dreamy days? They were great no doubt, but now they were over—brought to an abrupt curb by he, who permits. Yes, they were over like that song.

..Over for her and for her little angel. Yea, they were doomed....Anyhow, the mother at least, had had her initial joys....The little angel would have none! She would never have the pleasure of joining a group singing at the beach. She would never experience a dalliance from any boy....Indeed! It would be better if she were dead!

Luzia sat by her daughter and said her prayers. The little girl was fast asleep, yet now and then scratching her neck....Perhaps a mosquito bite.

She got up, put on her old silk night-gown and sat again on the bed....The girl was breathing lightly....Her hand was still scratching....

"Serla," she whispered lovingly, "You shouldn't scratch the whole time. Otherwise your skin will be irritated and you'll have a 'bub'." And slowly, without disturbing her, she put aside the hand that had been scratching; saying in her usual motherly manner. "Sleep, my...." What she saw started her. She got up hurriedly, lit the candle again, because the dim redness of the lamp wasn't enough to distinguish and returned to the bed. The little one was still sleeping, and her hands were as they had been after she'd put them aside—resting freely on the pillow. Luzia brought her face nearer and looked fixedly. There was a dark spot on her neck—a roundish dot about the size of a plum, a little redish in tint. Just like the one her father'd had six months before the other symptoms followed. The child was hardly one then.

She cursed within her breath as she gasped "God Again!.... Permits!!.... How stupid! Serla," she screamed in an urgent and broken voice "when did you have this?" The child woke up with a start. "What mu....?" And then she saw her mother biting her lips in an effort to control pointing to the dark spot on the front side of her neck. "It's nothing, mummy," she said innocently, "It's just scratching and burning....For many days I've had this, mummy". And to suggest duration she pushed back her head and pointed vacantly above her head, saying "I don't remember....Why, mummy, are you going to give me medicine?"

"Yes, my little angel. I shall give you the tears of a mother." The child did not comprehend, poor thing! Suddenly, looking at the grave eyes of her mother, she said "Am I going to die, mummy?"

Luzia stared blankly at the innocence of those words. Yet, silly though they were they had some deep meaning. At least to a mother.

"Yes, my child" she replied "You're going to die, but not alone!"

"If I'm going to die, then I'll meet my dead father in Heaven, no mummy?"

So apparently foolish the words seemed, yet how philosophic. Really! "Yes, my love," she responded. And then a smile came to her lips, a smile of triumph, of that which was fading, crumbling under their—no, her feet, because she 'wanted' it so. She did not mind what she was letting fade behind her.

"My lovely, sherry" she said at last, kissing passionately the spot on her neck. "You will meet your dead father there—in the Land of the Dead....And among the dead, we shall live...."

The child did not understand. "Are you going to die too mummy?" she asked anxiously.

Luzia kissed her daughter again. "Yes, my child. Among the living, I shall die...."

"I don't understand...."

"You shall, my child...." She blew off the candle. And they slept—By the dimness of the red light of the lamp....

Chapter XXII

TEMPEST
Manuel C. Rodrigues

THERE is no place under the sun which a stranger cannot make his own. What is needed is time, adaptability and a natural tendency to make friends. But Pedro Antonio Entraciano Rogaciano de Almeida was entirely new to Bombay. He had been there only a month. A young man, 17 years old, just fresh from school, he had taken up a job in a commercial firm. But working from 8 o'clock in the morning till about 6-30 in the evening, sometimes later, he had no time at his disposal to explore the vicinity. He had no relatives in Bombay. He was friendless, and terribly lonely; in fact, quite sick of everything. When at school, he had been accustomed to all sorts of vigorous physical outdoor games—football, cricket, hockey, swimming and other kinds of sports that took him out into the open, in the exhilarating warmth of sun and air. But here, in this unknown place and with late hours in the office, he didn't know how to pass his time. Mental diversion? That was all right for sickly, consumptive book worms who have never yet known the healthy enjoyment a well developed body can experience. If these sedentary dreamers had only exercised their bodies and fallen passionately in love with Nature, he was sure, there would be no need for them to go to books and fill so many hospitals and asylums.

Revolving, like a young reformer, this great problem in his mind which he thought to be at the very root of so much unhappiness, he sat at the table and wrote a letter to his mother. It had to be done. He was not going to serve like a slave in an unappreciative, uncongenial atmosphere and kill the Man in him. He was going to chuck the job and start for Goa, immediately.

Bombay's climate did not agree with him. And, well, he wasn't keeping good health. In Goa he could live independent and free, master of his own house and soul. There was a small plot behind his house which could be enclosed with a fence and made to yield much. He could rear piglings there and poultry. He could also build up a small garden of flowers, fruit and all kinds of vegetables to be sold at the weekly market-day in the City.

But, on second thoughts, he tore the letter and sat down to write another. This time he explained to his mother how difficult it was, in the dingy hotel in which he lived, to get a warm water bath even once a week. How the morning and the evening tea which he had to gulp down with closed eyes like poison, was upsetting his liver. And, to worsen matters, the small room in which the hotel-keeper had huddled him together with a man much older than he, had only a small window overlooking somebody else's kitchen. In such a place he could not take his usual breathing exercises. Nor could he play his fiddle in the nights. His neighbour thundered that his child was sick or that he could get no sleep. The hotel-keeper to complained that he was raising the electric bill by burning the light too far into the night. He therefore requested his old mother, on receipt of this letter, to come to Bombay. He was going to look for a nice little house somewhere in the suburbs. They said living was cheap there. He would also try and send her some money for the journey.

He wrote the letter, read it with satisfaction and enclosed it in an addressed envelope. But some indescribable feeling overpowered him. He shed a few tears, tore the letter into many bits and watched them float down from the fourth story— aimlessly. Some fell into the neighbour's kitchen, some into the lane, others were swept away by the wind.

He stood there for a while, motionless as a statue, looking out of the window. The street lamps were lit. Beneath their dim lights many a passerby showed his face for a while and disappeared. From his neighbour's clock he heard 11 o'clock strike. His room-mate was away, and he was alone. With a sudden impulse he dressed himself up, switched off the light and quietly slipped out of the room. The proprietor's dog on the stairs barked at him, but soon, recognising the familiar voice, got out of his way. He went down the stairs and out into the night, his heart throbbing fast with a strange delight and expectation. Outside, the atmosphere was cool and quiet as though some invisible arms were holding him in a trance. He shook himself up and walked fast—his heart beating faster—down the lane and out into the open road dodging the full blaze of a car here and the movements of a policeman there. Somewhere on the cold pavement a young mother nursing her child became conscious of his stare and pulled the insufficient cloth on her body on to her breast. He changed his direction, and moved towards a house whose half-screened windows threw out dancing shadows, patches of light, fragrance, laughter and music. He paused, hesitant, like one who might be familiar with the house but knew not its inmates. From outside he listened to the gramophone music, for a long while. A loud Fox-Trot was followed by a hectic Rumba and then a sleepy Waltz. He turned away swiftly. Music had sharpened the pain in his being. He was intoxicated, drugged. Walking quickly down the road and over the railway bridge he came into the Charni Road Gardens. The moon was just peeping out shyly from behind a cloud, revealing underneath the dense foliage swaying to the rhythm of the breeze. With a sudden thrill he perceived a vast green lawn sparkling moist with dew in the midst of which many-coloured flowers seemed to sip their own fragrance. He felt he heard whispers among the trees in the dark. Feeling his way across the black shadows he slipped over a stone and fell. Some dry leaves and a tender shoot of a plant cracked under his weight. He felt ashamed; and no less frightened. When he got up, everything was quiet. He ran away madly towards the Marine Drive. Tired, he sat on the dike and watched the calm ocean snoring like a mighty giant in his sleep. He felt he must do something; shout, cry or sing. The waters were dancing under the moonlight, like visions in a dream. Far away, he heard the sound of a wave roll down towards him. It came nearer and nearer, heaved its bosom, sighed like a lover, lapped the wall under his feet, chuckled and retired.

The sea looked friendly and inviting. Should he strip his clothes, take a cool plunge into the sea, swim a few yards and come back? But that part of the night, when there are no people about he might be suspected of attempting suicide. No, he was not prepared to go to gaol. Heavily he turned back and entered a restaurant. He was attracted there by a crowd of onlookers. There was the weekly public dance. The admission was free. So he sat at the table and ordered some cold drinks. Knowing no one, and too proud to risk a refusal, he must watch others dancing.

Somewhere nearby, a girl was seated alone sipping a glass of beer. Their eyes met. She smiled. He was surprised, but smiled in return. Maybe they had been introduced before. She finished her glass, lit a cigarette, got up and slowly passed by him. But he was too shy to speak to her. He sat recollecting where he could have known her. However much he searched his memory he could not remember having met her anywhere. Determined, nevertheless, to make her acquaintance and incidentally ask her for a dance, he went out, not without a tinge of nervousness. But she had found a friend and was gone! Overcome with strange emotions, he left the place and went straight to the hotel. On entering his room, he switched on the light, changed his clothes and physically exhausted, dropped into his bed like a stone.

But when sleeping, as he came to know next morning, he had forgotten to put out the light.

Chapter XXIII

THE AESTHETE
(A monologue)
Armando Menezes

I AM *the* Aesthete. The accent is on 'I am quite as much as on 'Aesthete'. For the Aesthete alone truly and vividly *is*. The rest of mankind merely exist.

I am, therefore, not at all surprised that some owlish member of that inextinguishable tribe of Philistines placed me in the gallery of Oddities. I was *never* annoyed at the soulless, heavy-footed stupidities of the mere moralist and utilitarian.

Why, I am not odd at all! I am the only normal man; though my sheer normality does set me more than a little apart from the common herd of men that, as Tennyson's Ulysses says,

'*Hoard, and sleep, and feed, and know not me!*'

There was a celebrated ancestor of mine, named Oscar Wilde, whose brilliance stuck in the gullets of the Philistines, whose sublime effrontery made them shrivel and dry up in their pachydermatous skins. He had a weakness—a *penchant* shall I say?—for certain flowers; and that was enough for the whole pack of philistines! One man thought he had hit him off in a book called *The Green Carnation*. Another was inspired to compose an entire opera in which Wilde was represented as walking down Piccadilly with a poppy or a lily in his medieval hand.

It shows how completely out poor Gilbert was in his grasp of the aesthetic idea. The true Aesthete does not care for lilies at all. What he is after is the pure and disembodied *idea* of the lily—its stark liliness so to say. With that great aesthete, James

Elroy Flecker, he holds that Beauty lives though lilies die. A flower—whether it is a poppy or a lily, a sunflower or a green carnation—is, to him, only a means to an end: to a button-hole, for instance.

And yet, the Aesthete submits to the voluptuous fascination of flowers. If, like that legendary Indian tribe recorded by Pliny, he could live solely on the scent of flowers, he would. That is why no meal is complete for me without an exquisitely composed flower-vase. In fact, when I have a very special guest, I depend for the evening's success not on my cook but on my gardener. When I smoke—an occasional but expensive cigar—it is mostly for the delicious pleasure of watching the diaphanous smoke-rings I blow in the air.

Only the finest of pleasures will content me: the clarity of form; the purity of colour; the elusive light; the last subtle shade; sensation simply as sensation, unweighed with purpose, even with meaning. When Rossetti (Dante Gabriel, you know) writes that the Blessed Damozel, in the cold infinities of Heaven, made warm the gold bar she leaned on, I like to think that even in Heaven there shall be sensation. when the old poet calls my attention to

A winning wave, deserving note,
In the tempestuous petticoat',

I like that too. I duly note the winning wave. But I deplore the 'tempestuous'. It gives me the shudders. It makes me literally sea-sick. Beauty should be calm. I like calm sensations.

I cultivate a vibrant serenity—which, unfortunately, dull people mistake for superiority. When I see mobs and mobs of earnest men and women milling around as if they were hoping to catch any moment a glimpse of the Holy Grail, I smile. It is not a superior smile. For that matter, it is hardly a smile. I am beyond both pity and laughter. They are both so middle-class! In the translucent medium of my contemplation, there is nothing for tears; not for irony either. All's either ineffably beautiful, or else unspeakably ugly. I sudder but I do not condemn. That would

The Aesthete

be horribly undignified and—respectable. It would mean that I accepted the values of the rabble. *Nil admirari* is my motto, if you know what I mean. I always find explanations tiresome and condescending. In the daily strife, the immortal Tallerand's *pas de zele*. But, really, I do not strive at all. That would be infinitely tiresome, too, and middle-class. In my nirvana of pure consciousness, there is no place for striving. I hardly even dare to live: as another aesthete remarked, I leave it to the servants (of whom, for the moment, I have none).

But though I am loath to strive, I am nothing if not intense. I have therefore nothing but contempt for people like Max Beerbohm, who thought that estheticism consisted in gentle posturings and wavings of hands. I allow that our gestures are aesthetically satisfying; that is because we cultivate beauty in all things; but they are no index of the intensity of the soul within, incessantly rapt in contemplation of all that is fine and serene. That is why we seem content with little sins. Little sins are best, provided they are new. It is the sensation of the sin that matters, not it content; not certainly its gains and losses. All sickness is to me an obscene misdemeanour. Poverty is merely inartistic. Death, only a bore—unless, of course, it is violent enough to give a new *frisson,* a new sensation.

But these words mean nothing to the Philistine—or the votary of what one of my ancestors called 'that harsh, uncomely puritanism'. That is why I prefer to use words that mean nothing—though in a sense they mean everything to the sensitive and finely-attuned spirit. That is why, too, I repudiate with all the fervour of my intense soul that despicable libel on all aesthetes: that they have nothing to say, and say it beautifully! The *bourgeoisie* have everything to say, and *how* they say it! Say it over and over again—without *nuances,* without obliquity, without overtones—until all meaning is pawed out of each word—

'*Lost angel of a ruined Paradise!*'

My profundity can only be translated into aphorisms. My small talk is a volley of coruscating epigrams. I communicate through paradox; or through silence (if ever silence does occur to me).

There is a notion among the dilettantes of art and literature that the Aesthete is a precious Dandy, affecting the loudest and most unfashionable dress, and nursing in the secret night the most adorable and spurious of love-locks. That is only a delusion. The true Aesthete is in external detail, the most austere of creatures. Today, he rather favours the bush-shirt. A little *distingue,* perhaps, in his taste; a little bizzarre;—but only to put the Philistine in his place. Open-collared—to assert his personal freedom. A beard, if one *can* grow a beard. He doesn't go in either, for rare and strange stimulants—except, perhaps, just once—to sample a new sensation.

And when he comes to organize his sensations, he calls it his Culture. I burn with a hard gem-like flame, with Walter Pater. I murmur to myself again and again all he has said about the *Mona Lisa.* I am in the vanguard of all literary and artistic movements. I once dreamt of scent-organs, with Huysmans; of vicious negresses, with Baudelaire; of absinthe and hashish with—I forget whom. to-day, I converse in a slow deliberate manner, in a voice dark with innuendoes, of surrealism and abstract art and the stream of consciousness. The Pre-Raphaelite Movement moves me no longer. Picasso and all his works are *vieux jeux.* But give me Barque and Paul Klee! Give me the Ninth Symphony! Give me the unutterable Sartre—or even the Angry Young Men, the Beatniks and Beatles!....Yet, I have no time for books, except the slimmest. But give me a copy of the early Tennyson, or the later Keats, bound in limp Morocco, peacock green or ultramarine-blue, to feel it against my cheek—delicious softness against even more delicious softness!

But whenever I am laid up in bed, or my coterie of admirers have deserted me on a market day, or to see something vulgar like *My Fair Lady,* I love to skim the pages of an old favourite poem or essay—De Quincey's *Murder as one of the Fine Arts;* or the poem where the Bishop orders his tomb, in Browning:

Peach-blossom marble all, the rare; the ripe
As fresh-poured red wine of a mighty pulse!;

or that galloping tale of the friar artist who turned from pallid Madonnas to mark the Prior's buxom niece. When I am fatigued with new sensations, I lean back on my velvet cushions to murmur:

'And still she slept an azure-lidded sleep,
In blanched linen, smooth and lavendered,
While he forth from the closet brought a heap
Of candied apple, quince and plum and gourd,
With jellies soother than the creamy curd ...!'

When I have talked to a woman, all I remember is the provocative curve of her cheek, or the flutter of her dainty eyelashes. I have no time for strenuous heroes of earnest reformers. When I go to a temple, it is only to look at the architecture. And I love to recall the story of that medieval monk who, dying, pushed back the crucifix from his lips because it was not beautiful.

Chapter XXIV

THE FORSAKEN SON
J. M. Fernandes

THE Wireless Operator after sounding the weatherman over the telephone, switched off the hand-gear below this table. Simultaneously, the red tower lights of the two powerful transmitters went dead. The weather had been bad throughout the night and you couldn't transmit nor receive a single message.

"What, no schedule?" asked the second shift operator who had just walked into the small wireless room to take over.

"Heavy statics, Pete. The key is as useless as the mike. The signals are piling up and Tom Brime, the new Communications Superintendent, was himself here. I don't know when the ether will clear." So saying, Yakub turned round in his revolving chair, removed his head phones, and stretched out his legs. "Well, there begins another day for you!"

His short, curly-haired companion did not speak. He had turned about the modulator of the airconditioner and was looking out through the closed glass window, sad and pensive. That was one of Pete Sequeira's characteristics. He would often remain pensive and silent as if his mind and soul was detached from the immediate reality of his surroundings. But that morning he appeared to be exceptionally different.

Yakub poured the last cup of warm cocoa from the thermos into two paper cups and then, pushing one towards Pete, asked "What's wrong?"

There was still no reply. But Pete picked up the paper cup all right and after gulping down the sweet, chocolate-flavoured liquid, dropped himself into a spare chair. "Hell, Yakub....I'm sorry. I was just not myself."

It was too early to ring for the *farrash,* as the Arab peons are called. So, Yakub himself pulled the two paper cups together and gently threw them into the waste paper drum. "Say, I always notice you with that distant look in your eyes brooding over something." He remarked and then added. "What is it? Love, Money or Ambition?"

Pete looked inquiringly at Yakub for a moment wondering what poor Yakub might have been guessing about himself. Yakub's was certainly a happy life, not like his own. There was his wife from whom every mail from Lahore brought a letter, and there were the relatives and friends he so often warmly spoke about. How he wished he himself had a circle of relations and a home like that! After all, he reasoned, a man's success largely depends on his fellow man; good surroundings; proper circumstances and above all a good home. He smiled. "You're too curious, Yakub," said he and then himself added "Quite naturally."

A moment of silence might have passed between the two before Pete Sequeira spoke again. "You know, life is a pleasant experience for those who have everything they think they ought to have. Beyond that, it becomes a problem. In fact it is a conflict, a fight for existence, as they say. I tell you, there are many people without an ideal, or so much as even ambition, and they are just content to accept the world as it is. But there is that other person, the cynical and the questioning type, who often revolts against the scheme of things, sets up a goal for himself and goes about attaining it. Everything is against him; obstructions and hurdles innumerable. He is the centre of conjecture, envy, admiration and all that. As for himself, he is seldom happy and mostly unhappy. Do you get me Yakub? I know you'll call me philosophical. But then I wanted to make my life beautiful. Perhaps I have no right, or have I?"

His brows knit in attention. Yakub looked at him in half

curiosity, half humour and even a slight wonder and then, casually, sympathetically, remarked, "You're not happy over here, are you?"

Pete nodded his head. "I should have been in Europe by now, doing the things I always wanted to do as well as make the life of the very people who complain about me happier, easier and successful. Perhaps fortune has not decreed it although I have not been asking for the moon!"

There was tireless urge in Pete, one could easily sense that. For a wireless operator, he was educated, intelligent and helpful. Everyone liked his work and there were a few who secretly envied him. "If you don't feel like working," said Yakub, "I'll continue the shift. Go and enjoy yourself or sleep it off. You should be all right tomorrow."

"No, thanks," remonstrated Pete. Yakub could go off and he would look after the schedules. After the night's work, Yakub needed a good bath and rest. "Don't you worry about me," said Pete. "I'm perfectly all right. In fact, top o' the morning!"

A draft of hot air blew inside the airconditioned cubicle as Yakub, minutes after, left the lone operator to clear the bunch of signals, weather permitting.

Pete pulled out a friend's letter he had received the previous day saying the old servant woman had died back at home and memories flashed past his mind. The old man had died two years ago and now, the servant. Poor thing! The woman had served them well in times of stress and had laid great hopes on him. Now she was dead. Pete had no motor. The only faint recollection he had was that of her lying in bed and he was asked to kneel down and pray to God so that she might live. That happened when his sister Anna was born. The infant had survived the mother and, for all he knew, was probably a teenager now. Only he hadn't seen her for a long, long time.

It was a cruel scheme of things into which he had found himself. Despite the great love and attachment he had for his home, in Goa, his widower father's behavior had driven him away from it. Pete had started to work early in life and he recollected how he had specifically come to Bombay with a view to earn and learn at the same time. He had ambition. But the family had no means, and father, idling the best part of his life at home without any work, had dragged the palatial home into debt, want and humiliation.

Time passed. Pete stood up the strain very much an unwanted and unloved man. There are such things as appreciation, love, friends, relations, sympathy and understanding on which a man survives. But Pete had none.

But just as the uncared and untended tree grows in the forest; just as Joseph prospered in the land of Egypt sold by his own brothers—the hand of God rewarded Pete's diligence and want of blemish. He had leaned, nearly achieved his goal, and was independent. Security and future could take care of themselves now. He was no longer uncertain of tomorrow. He was free. Only he would have achieved much more if he had a proper people for a family and a good home. Money, the very thing that had brought about the separation, was there amply now. But the mischief had been done. Hearts had been broken, hopes lost, harmony and happiness of a home thrown to the winds due to a lack of understanding and appreciation from people who ought to have known better.

What was he to do now? the poor woman had died. She had been more than a mother to the motherless children, one of whom was Pete. He had vowed he would reward her devotion by making her happy, but no. Fate had not decreed it. He remembered her sulkiness when he and father had refused to sit at the same dining table. When food was short in the home and there was no money to buy it, she had pawned her own jewelry to buy the grain. It was father who had done it all. He had messed up everything. And Pete did not want to make the old man unhappy for the remaining few days of his life....

Suddenly the telephone rang. "Hello?" It was the weather office. "Is Yakub there?"

The voice on the other end said they were hoping the weather would turn to normal again by sunset. He could try the receivers by noon again, if he would like?

"Roger, Bud!" pete would do that.

With a sharp jerk the switchgear was put on again that afternoon and the red and green lights of the wireless equipment began to flicker again. The Marconiphone developed a faint note to a shrill tone as the circuits began to warm up. At last you could hear some distant voice on the usual frequency with readability too weak for copy. The changing to alternate channels brought no improvement either. But the weatherman had forecast the weather would improve. He thought he would try the machines later that evening again.

Chapter XXV

THE ROOT OF ALL EVIL
J. M. Fernandes

AFTER picking up his airbag and the thermos flask, Hubert again made sure he had not forgotten anything in the aircraft. He checked below his seat and then looked around. A white and blue envelope under the seat of an adjoining row of slumberettes met his eyes. He picked it up and made for the ramp.

A tall, mustached, turbaned Police Officer of the Karachi Emigration Department along with a hefty, short and smartly dressed airlines agent were waiting for him at the entrance of the airport building to check his papers and take him to the rest house until the connecting aircraft came along.

He had been to Karachi before, but never by an airplane. As the motor-coach took the passengers to the BOAC Birdhouse, which stands only a short distance from the airport, he wondered whether Karachi was not a better city seen from her airport than from her seaport. She was definitely cleaner land daintier here than there. The coach passed many a camel driven cart, a few cycle rickshaws, and many, many women in burkhas. It was nearly one o'clock and he was feeling hungry. He looked at the rear of the coach to make sure his suitcase was there.

At the resthouse a valet took him to his suite, put a freshly laundered towel in the bathroom and handed over to him a huge key with an equally huge wooden attachment with the suite number inscribed on it. Hubert could take a bath if he liked and then come to the dining hall by walking first to the left and then straight to the right. Lunch was ready but Hubert made sure he had locked the room before he left it. The immaculately dressed bearer was certainly efficient as he left with a salute and a smile on his face.

A hurried hot bath and a fresh set of clothes from his suitcase. As he was locking up the suit he thought he must have a drink today. Where was that Pakistani money had had brought with him? He looked into his jacket pockets and then into the airbag—there it was. A note of ten and a note of five Pakistani rupees. The open envelope he had found in the aircraft was also beside it. He pulled out the papers. There was no name, no address on the envelope. what were they? A cheque for Rs. 15,029 on the Universal Bank Limited, and a small handwritten note in Portuguese.

It read...."My dear Babu. In case anything happens to me, this money is for you and Baezinha. But do not spend it. Keep it as a standby only to be used for any illness or calamity. It took me some time and ingenuity to earn it. It has not been God-sent. This is not to say that I do not believe in God. I do. But I do not believe in people who place too much faith in God and make no honest effort to better their lot. Try and believe first in yourself that you can do something and work hard and God will bless you. It is easy to find excuses. It is easier still to spend money that you never earned or will ever earn. Because I believe this I have been made the black sheep of the house while they broke it down and ruined it after Mama died. I did my best to salvage whatever I could. Now you do the rest if you can. Love....Lucia."

Hubert bit his lip and hunger again reminded him. The handwriting was nice. the cheque was bearer? He looked at it again. It was crossed. It was signed "L. Neves." A peculiar name, wasn't it? The valet had said first to the left and then to the right. He walked to find the dining hall. There it was. He must have been late. Only a few people filled the huge hall of the rest house.

After studying the menu, Hubert ordered some whisky and soda and settled down to his lunch. He wondered why he didn't hand over the envelope to the hostess in the first place as he was getting down the ramp. At any rate, the owner implied a Goan lady passenger. But then he recalled he hadn't seen any Goan passengers in the aircraft during his journey from Bombay to Karachi. There was no other clue whatever. He had better trace out who the owner was. He gulped down the clear, piquant wine and cut at the huge morsel of beef while the waiter looked on. There was something intriguing about the message. God, money and self-confidence, puff!

It was not difficult to trace out who "L. Neves" was. She was the same lady sitting in the row opposite to his seat whom he took to be a South Indian. He recalled the moment when the aircraft was bending low over Juhu trying to gain height and he had looked about the faces of other passengers and found her with moist eyes as if about to cry. "I found something," he said. "Is it yours?" He handed over the envelope containing the note and the cheque. "Very kind of you," she replied recognizing the contents. "Thanks."

He eyed her for a while and said, "How strange, you don't even look like a Goan!" It was nearly 4 o'clock of the afternoon. He hadn't had his tea yet. Say, she spoke Portuguese and he was a total stranger around the place. Would she have tea with him? He would like to talk to her. A moment of hesitation, but she agreed. She would.

A huge cloud study graced the wall opposite. The concealed lighting gave it an added effect. The tune of a western opera was faintly audible. Where was she from and where was she going to? There was no reply. He added two more cubes from the sugar pot and sipped the mixture for taste. The coffee was no good. The toast too burned.

"I'm going to Kuwait, and you?" she asked after some time.

"To Dusseldorf for a six months' training on how to fire filaments. We in India want to make practically everything but our know-how and skill is very poor and the manufacturers abroad do not bother to tell us details. Never been out to the Continent before. I hear the pay is good in Kuwait?"

"Maybe. But I have taken up a job as governess. Four hundred rupees a month all found including shelter and transport," she said. "It's an American household. I didn't want to go at first....considerations of money, you know?" She had tried everything in India from nursing to teaching and from a typist to a receptionist.

"I understand," remarked Hubert. "You have no brothers?"

Lucia had a brother. But he was a waster and, like dad, an old fashioned man. He had stuck to one job because he believed like everyone else a man should never be a rolling stone even if it didn't pay one in the long run. They were altogether four of them, two brothers and two sisters—orphans with nothing to fall back on plus a very hostile, mean and curious set of relatives. Money was necessary, and plenty of it, if they were to survive. It was no use believing God takes care of everything...."

"Why are you such a non-believer in God?" At last Hubert was coming round the point. "When I read your note, it struck me why you wrote it and what had shaken your faith in God. It was very strange to one brought up in a Catholic home, especially since you are a lady."

"God? I believe in Him all right. But tell, is it a crime to possess money and live well? Can you help yourself or anyone without it! Well, charity itself begins with it. I would rather die rich than poor in this world, if I can help it. Look around you, Gentleman.

..More than money, poverty is the root of all evil—there is no harm in earning and spending money the right way?"

something was welling inside Hubert's throat and he coughed. He was wondering whether he was talking to a woman, a business tycoon, or to a priest. He glanced at her again, this time particularly. That small neck with a thick gold chain around it; that sensitive outline of moving lips with a light touch of lipstick; a delicate earlobe with a faint trickle of gold wire suspending what looked like an art pearl. He recalled having read Dickens, Maurois, Tolstoy, Hazlitt and Gorky hammering at the reality of life, wealth, religion and poverty in relation and poverty in relation to money down the ages. What was this now? He puffed deep at his freshly filled pipe and looked at the yellow metal ring on the little finger of his own left hand to make sure it was there and then uttered his thoughts unconsciously, audibly. "He'd be a lucky man who'd take you for a wife!"

"What!"

"I was saying few women have enough sense in them." And then to distract her attention he inquired, "Babus must be the youngest of the two brothers?"

While she nodded in affirmation, Hubert's mind took him back to Alice and the young one at home. For Alice money was to be spent all and more of it, if she could find it. It was a vicious circle, a bourgeois neighbourhood in which they lived—all middle class. What would Alice do if something happened to him? There was an Insurance Policy he had made. But she was not the working type. She quarreled with everything and everyone. Relations? Pooh! They were worse than friends, only to enjoy, to pass time. Even a big legacy wouldn't help Alice. She wouldn't know how to use it.

The Constellation that took Hubert was the earlier to come that night. They dined together and purchased a few picture postcards. Hubert explained, "My little one would love to see these camels. You know, he's quick at learning." At the customs gate she gave him a warm handshake and he looked deep into her eyes. Would they meet again? Hubert joked air travel was quite safe nowadays.

"*Seja feliz,* Lucia, and may God bless you."

Chapter XXVI

PINKY'S MOTHER
V. Sivaramakrishnan

It is spring-time in Goa. Nature is in one of her exuberant moods. Clothed in green, she is radiant with a freshness all her own. The mango, arching over the highway, is a riot of yellow. The fragrant blossoms in bunches smile a welcome to the traveller.

"Mai! Mai!!" Rose stretched herself languidly over the mat and called her mother.

"Get up, Rosie, get up".

"Mai, how can you milk all the buffaloes yourself? Who will get you water from the well? And then to feed *them!* Who will do it, Mai, who will?" The girl went on prattling in sing-song Konkani.

"Don't bother about it all, dear. Get up, wash yourself".

The mother looked lovingly at her daughter. 'Poor thing, she is worried about me when she should have more happy thoughts', she muttered to herself as her frail bosom heaved and a sign escaped from her mouth.

Rose was in no mood to get up. She stared vacantly at the roof. There were question-marks all over, everywhere.

'Who will feed the Dukor?'—this thought came bubbling up her mind more than once. How she liked feeding them, the sow and her litter, ten in all, every day! She would be ambling along with her brood, grunting and sniffing the earth, somewhere, unseen. But the moment Rose shouted 'Yo, yo', the whole lot of them would come running and crowd around her. Pinky, the one of that colour, was the smartest and seemed to be more fond of Rose than the others. How he would wind himself round her legs and prick her soft calf muscles with his bushy back!

Rose had a charming way with all, man or beast. Perhaps, it was her smile that won old Blackie's brood over to her. Else, how could they be so little afraid of her? The timidity of these creatures is to be seen to be believed. You can see through their small, dark eyes their mortal fear of man. They would shy away at your footfall and sometimes, in utter confusion, moving this way and that, run through your legs!

"Rosie, get up". The mother's voice was now peremptory. She would be the last woman to let the love for her daughter get the better of a stern sense of duty. Past fifty, she herself had known no respite from hard work since the day she joined her man.

It was a family of twelve that she looked after. There were besides buffaloes to be cared for and pigs to be reared. At the peep of dawn she would be in the pen milking the buffaloes, six of them, with bursting udders. She would herself have the milk filled up in bottles—there are brandy bottles enough and to spare in Goa—and arrange for their dispatch. Her man would take them round; sometimes she herself would have to go.

From the pen to the kitchen. Breakfast should be got ready—baked bread and tea. And then to the market for fish and mutton or vegetables. Back home, the pigs should be fed and the fish cut and cooked for the midday meal. Meal over, the pots should be scrubbed clean and the floor swept. When could she then relax? If relax she did, Rosie was sure to come scratching her scraggy hair. Taking her head on her lap, she would pick out the lice one by one and smash them with her fingernails.

"Maw, Maw"—that would be the signal for attending to the buffaloes again. Milking, bottling the milk, feeding the pigs, drawing water from the well, cooking—the routine would go on till late in the night. A hurried bath, a quick meal and then....tired eyelids would close upon tired eyes.

So the woman bore the burden and heat of the day.

Tender of limb, she was strong of will. Of course, she leaned a little on her daughter when the latter came of age. Though inclined to be lazy, Rose braced herself up when it came to helping her poor, little mother. Rose could bargain, too, over the pigs with better luck than her mother.

The man, father of ten, was a waster content of count his money and lose it at the *taverna*. The boys were no better. They were dandys to boot with a flair for the twist.

"Rosie, get up. You can't be the child of your mother all your life. You are becoming the wife of a man".

The girl was already betrothed. Jose, the carpenter, who lived nearby, was the bridegroom. The wedding day was drawing near.

Rosie's house was full of bustle and animation. A sewing machine whirred all day and spawned gay frocks and plain petticoats. Women chattered and girls giggled. Liquor arrived in caskets and the men sat around, drinking, smoking, joking and laughing. They were merry, as merry as the waves of the sea.

Suddenly the swines shrieked in unison. Pinky was squealing its life out. Blackie's brood was running helter-skelter, dodging a pack of barking dogs and a man with a jute bag. It was a scene of terror in the drama of death. Pinky was well-fed and he would make for a good feast on the wedding day. The man was out to catch it.

★ ★ ★

Bells pealed and crackers exploded, proclaiming Jose and Rose as man and wife. Friends and relatives watched and solemn ceremony at the altar of the neat, little Church in silence and reverential awe.

Rose's mother was not there. She was at work as usual— milking the cows, drawing water from the well, feeding the pigs, cooking, scrubbing and sweeping. Her face was swollen and her eyes bulging—she had been crying for long. Her dear daughter was going away and away from her. Even the men had turned their faces when the mother and daughter, locked in a tight embrace, sobbed before the carriage took the bride to the Church. Over her arched brow stood the brooding thought of separation.

"Yo, yo". She could but feebly raise her voice. The pigs came running along from nowhere, the voracious eaters! No, Blackie was standing aloof. Her frightened eyes glistened. A streak ran across her snouty face. She, the mother of Pinky, was brooding! The smart pig was gone she knew not where. She had none to console her in her inexpressible grief.

★ ★ ★

The mango blossoms over the highway had turned black—such is the sacrifice demanded of a mother in confinement. A few small, green mangoes peeped out of the foliage. 'Plop' fell one when struck with a stone by an urchin on the roadside.

Chapter XXVII

FEAR OF DEATH
Ravindra Kelekar

Two girls sat talking. One of them was a sailor's daughter, the other a batkar's. While they talked the sailor's daughter asked the batkar's daughter, "Tomorrow I am going in a katamarine to catch fish. You coming?"

"What? In the sea? Not me *bai*.... I am scared...." she said.

"Scared?....Scared of what? I always go" the sailor's daughter replied. Even so the batkar's daughter did not muster the courage to go with her. They dropped the matter there and started talking about something else. From one subject they moved to another till the sailor's daughter started to tell how her grand father had died, "My grandfather was on a ship. While going to Rangoon he was caught in a storm. The ship was wrecked, grandfather drowned and died."

Batkar's daughter's eyebrows rose and she asked:

"If that's so how does your father go on the ships?"

"What do you mean, how? We are people who live on ships" she replied.

"But isn't he scared?"

"Why should he be? Sailors are not afraid of storms", she said.

Well, tell me something, what was your grandfather's father doing?

"He was also a fisherman".

"How did he die?" Batkar's daughter asked.

"He also drowned and died" she said.

160

"And his father."

"He also died the same way" the fisherman's daughter said.

"My, my what sort of people you are I don't understand" Batkar's girl exclaimed in surprise. The sailor's daughter thought for a while. Then she asked the batkar's girl:

"Your grandfather recently passed away. What happened to him?"

"He was old....One day it was cold and on waking up in the morning we found he had passed away while asleep in bed" she said.

"Well, your great grandfather, how did he die?"

"He also died in bed in his sleep."

"And great great grandfather?"

"I was told he also died the same way."

"Oh my God! All died in bed while asleep? Even then every night you sleep in your bed....how is it you are not afraid?" What could the batkar's girl reply?

Transdlated from Konkani
by Luis S. R. Vas

Chapter XXVIII

THE SLIP
Louis Gracias

EVEN in callow youth, when those of my age were sportive and carefree and not a whit concerned about the world they lived in, I have wished I could change "this sorry scheme of things entire". Yes, even then it struck me that "God's in His Heaven, but all is wrong wth the world."

Woman has meant much to me. Perhaps it is because I have had no mother, having lost her when I was just a babe. Perhaps only a woman can appease the hunger of my soul: an all-devouring and an all encompassing hunger. Perhaps—who knows?—God has unveiled to me the mystery of *what* He made and what we carelessly call *woman*.

I was only fifteen at the time. But since then experience has joined to experience like the links of an endless chain, discovering all that is low and sordid, depraved and disgusting, tragic and terrible.

If I had always loved to disregard my father's cherished admonishious, it was, I suppose, because the prime-eval fascination to break the given order had been unduly infused in me. I smoked and drank: I read all sorts of proscribed literature.

Yes, I was only a lad of fifteen then. Impressions at that receptive age, it is said, endure forever. No wonder, it is all so fresh and vivid, so forceful and fearful, even today two and twenty years after....

One evening decked out like a man, with a boy's fancy to be considered older than his years, I was safely installed in a corner of the Cafe R— at Byculla. I was drinking beer, that delicious, frothy, refreshing beverage.

I was drinking it in greedy sips, when a woman suddenly entered. It was across the snowy summit of my newly replenished glass that I descried her.

Standing in the centre of the cafe, she cast vague glances at the men all round. Then looking terribly hurt and grieved, she moved slowly and undecidedly towards me and dropped listlessly into a seat at a table directly next to mine.

She looked completely worn and torn. And all about her seemed to hover a sense of frustration and fatality.

Somehow my gaze was drawn towards her: an intent gaze, perplexed and painful.

The bridge of her nose had given way. Her cheeks were hollow; her bosom straight and flat; and her figure bent, like one whose shoulders are bowed with weight.

Yet her small ovel face bore dim traces of beauty, like a mocking memory. And in her glance, half sad and half desperate, there lingered still a touch of tenderness—the glimmer of the soul of a woman.

She would not drink. Nor did the waiters care to come to her. They only kept looking at her, and then whispered something to each other and smiled mysteriously.

Occasionally she would glance at the men drinking, with a perfunctory smile, her eyes full of vague promises. But none of them seemed interested or concerned.

Some fifteen minutes elapsed in this manner. Then, suddenly, the head waiter, a sour-faced, impudent man, strutted across to the woman. "Go away!" he cried out. "If you don't we'll call the police. How often must you be told, we serve drinks here?"

To me a woman is a woman. She was so even when I was a child. She was all the more so when I grew up into a precious boy and could reason about her like any man. I could never flatter a man for being chivalrous. It is his duty to be so, because of the woman who bore him; because of her who sprouted from the same old tree as he. It is a woman who will join hands with him in his life-long destiny. It is a woman, again, who will form part of his own flesh and blood.

The waiter, therefore, angered me. And pushing away my chair, I rose and accosted him.

"Hold your tongue, you dog," I said. "Or I'll teach you, do you hear?....The lady shall not leave."

The man stunned. He showed it in his eye and shuffling foot.

But soon there followed a wild burst of laughter. It proceeded in disgusting, Stentorian waves from all sides: a stormy proclamation of the folly of youth.

And my anger rose; so did my charity.

"Be-beasts!" I shouted at the men, glowing at them.

But they laughed all the louder.

Then the woman, growing suddenly bold, shouted in her turn:

"Beasts! that's what you are. You've had your fill. May your bones rot in your own filth, you devils!"

Her words seemed to have clipped off their tongues. Instantly an intense calm prevailed: a sepulchral stillness, adjudging all their laughter as only a condonation of their swinish guilt.

I turned towards her and smiled.

She signed and thanked me.

"Say, what will you have?" I said.

"Rum, please."

"And ginger?—or soda?"

She began tittering. "What a big man you are, really?" she said. "No. Rum, just rum, please."

I gave the order. Then fetching my glass, I sat beside her.

She was looking at me with a look of intense gratitude,

smiling. In her smile I saw the one sudden triumph of those who have known nothing but defeat and humiliation.

She swilled the rum with a smack, and then wiped her mouth with the back of her hand.

"One more, please—do you mind?" she said.

"Certainly not!" I said.

"What should I have done without drink and sleep?" she said, wondering.

"Why?"

"Don't you see?—sleeping, one forgets; so also, drunk."

"Forget what?" I said.

"Oh, you wouldn't understand!" She shook her head firmly. "Otherwise, it would certainly have been different!"

And she emptied the second glass as hurriedly as the first.

"What use is it being older than one's years?" she said. "As you are—or, as I was? The blood will remain what it is, so will the flesh".

I listened sorrowfully, mystified.

"How easy and thoughtless it was!" she said, in an awful undertone. "How common, my God!....Yet you have your name cancelled from the book of life—with not even a dog's chance!"

"Waiter," I called, under a sudden impulse. "An other rum and beer."

"You know?" she said. "Though I forever struggle to forget, all I do is remember—But why are you staring at me like that?"

What could I say? Misfortune had come to her, a terrible misfortune, when young. But *what* could I say?

"How was I different from the other girls who slip in the lustihood of their treacherous youth?" she said. "How? How?....One little slip, when dreaming I tell you; and all's gone up in smoke—hope, love, marriage, home, *everything!*"

She finished the third peg, and suddenly sank into silence and shadow.

Some minutes after, she resumed her speech, but she had turned off from herself.

She scanned me tenderly, lovingly, the way my sister or mother would have done. "But why do you come her, eh?" she said. "This isn't a spot for boys like you."

I nodded guiltily. I was overpowered by the realisation of what good might not have blossomed from this forlorn and unfortunate creature.

"My little man! why go out of your way to encounter misery?" she said. "Don't you know she does enough prowling and pouncing by herself?"

And I put my arm around her. Even the thought of my stalwart father could not deter me.

But she laughed as though she were tickled. "You must be mad!" she said. "What am I? — nothing but dead flesh, I tell you!"

How could I agree? "Nonsense!" I said. "You are good and beautiful—I love you"

All at once there was an unearthly sparkle in her eyes. Like an enraptured being, she suddenly seized me and covered my face with rapid, burning-hot kisses.

And I wept, wept bitterly and long. Yet, those were the first kisses a woman ever bestowed on me and the dearest and best I have ever had.

Through my tears, I seemed to see her as when she was young: a girl in her bloom; lovely and fascinating; gay, lithe and lively; kind and gentle; her life full of hopes and dreams. A girl whom any man would have proudly married. A wife who would have made a home, that very home which all men in their time devoutly pray for....

But just then the clock struck nine, and the cafe R—was closed for the day.

When I had paid off the score, there were only three annas

and two pice left in my little, brown, imitation leather purse purchased at the Bandra fair.

We moved along the footpath, slowly an silently, for quite a while. Our arms were tightly clasped round each other, protectively.

But as we came to the Victoria Gardens, my friend suddenly fixed her gaze skywards.

"It was night like this," she said, in a far-off voice in sympathy with events that were long past and irrevocable. "The same old moon was peeping from behind the tamarind tree, as it is now. And we two...exactly like this. We were returning from the pictures after the nine o'clock show. Miserable orphan! Cursed seventeen!... He was a handsome neighbour, kind and attentive, young and handsome, but corrupt — how the devil was I to know? In the sleepy light of the moon, his roving arm... God! that slip cost me everything! syphilis! *everything!*.... My uncle, my mother's sister's husband promptly cast me away. Ever since Auntie died he was swearing I was a burden on his hands. But *this* was too much for him....It was not *his* fault, but my fate!... And sensitive, forlorn and penniless as I was, what could I do?..."

In that question was the answer to her whole life: a virgin page splashed completely over by a bottle of black ink that had abruptly tilted-a page that could never be redeemed nor replaced!

"But what the hell am I doing here?" she suddenly asked herself, looking around incredulously, as though she had just woken from a dream. Then in less than a second, tearing away from me she was speeding across the Sussex Road: a ghost — a substanceless shadow!

Chapter XXIX

ROSALIA
Telo de Mascarenhas

WITH the Lyceum course behind them, Mrs. Lidia went with her son to visit Louis Bernardo's family, distant relatives, whom Carlos Manoel did not know yet.

Seeing Rosalia, with her oval golden face of 'madonna', framed with two black wings of hair, luminous and vivacious eyes, slender, smiling and vibrating with life like a string of violin, he fell suddenly in love with her, and his furtive glances were more expressive than the best lyrical poem.

During hiss student days Carlos Manoel had been a 'courreur des femmes'. But his past love adventures had left no sign nor caused damage to his heart. At this first encounter he stood distant and discreet without showing the innermost feelings that troubled his soul. But she, with her sixth feminine sense, guessed that she had caused some excitement in him. She did not acknowledge it and treated him with calm deference and simulated indifference.

It was very long since the two families had last met. But now that Carlos Manoel was in his late teens, he needed to be close to their relatives and to come out of the shell in which he always had lived. Mrs. Lidia wanted to introduce him to the relatives and not allow him to be unsociable like a wild animal. They were cordially welcomed by Louis Bernardo's family. "For a long time we have not seen you cousin", said Mrs. Lubelia, and addressing Carlos Manoel she added. "And you are now almost a man, thank God."

"Father, we have a surprise. Come and see who is here", said Rosalia to her father.

"Who is there?", asked Louis Bernardo coming out from his room, and exclaimed seeing the visitors. "How nice of you cousin Lidia. Only now did you remember that you have relatives in this corner of the world? And you Carlos Manoel, how are you? Who had seen you and who sees you now! You are grown up! Have you done well in your studies?"

"*Comme ci, Comme ca,* uncle. I have finished the Lyceum this year.

"Good, good. I am happy to hear this news."

Tea was served in the living room, while Mrs. Ubelia and Mrs Lidia sat down on the sofa exchanging their views.

"This is not a short visit, I hope. I hope you will stay at least for a week with us", said Mrs. Ubelia.

"It is impossible, believe me, cousin. I cannot leave the house for more than two days."

"How did you fare in your examination this year, Carlos Manoel?" asked Louis Bernardo.

"I did my best, uncle. I don't know whether you are aware that this year a bunch of new professors, all Goans, came from Lisbon. Some of them interrupted their studies to avail of the tide. It was a favour done by one of our influential politicians to fix his own relatives and friends in Lyceum, as is the current trend."

"Yes, I know some of them. How are they?"

"Well, to show off their petty knowledge they made themselves ferocious. There was a true murder of the innocents this year".

"What course you intend to take up next, Carlos Manoel? I hope you will not put an end to your studies with the Lyceum", asked Mrs Lubelia.

"In this country where there is not much to choose from,

aunty Lubelia, one can only be a doctor or a provisional advocate, like most of the people. I have opted for medicine. For lawyer or liar I have no ability."

"It is a good profession that helps bring the dying to life. Besides, I need a doctor in the family to cure my ailments", said Louis Bernardo jokingly.

"Family saints don't work miracles. In this country medical practitioners cannot make ends meet", said Carlos Manoel.

Rosalia at the instance of Mrs Lidia played Mendelson's pieces at the piano.

"Very well, very well. Our Rosalia is a great artist", said Mrs Lidia, applauding.

Carlos Manoel stood from his chair and very courteously congratulated her, saying: "Believe me, cousin Rosalia, I have never heard anybody play the piano as well as you. You are a *virtuoso*".

"It is very sweet of you, cousin. You are very kind. Thank you", she said laughing and blushing.

She went out of the living room to hide her emotion. She also was not indifferent to so affable a young man.

★ ★ ★

The next day, a Sunday, after breakfast, Rosalia asked Carlos Manoel: "Cousin, would you like to come to church with us?"

"Of course, Cousin Rosalia. I sometimes go to the dominical Mass".

The church was crowded. While the priest performed the Mass, at the choir the pupils of Schola-Cantorum chanted to the tune of the organ liturgical Hymns and pieces by Palestrina. Outside the church the sun shone gloriously over the sugarcane fields and the palm tree groves which filtered a green shadow on the pathways.

Returning from the church, Rosalia and Carlos Manoel walked side by side, followed by the two ladies and Maria Isabel, sister of Rosalia.

"I have a secret from you, Rosalia", said Carlos Manoel looking at her directly as he wanted to read her inner feelings.

"A secret for me? I don't know to keep secrets".

"A secret which concerns only the two of us. A secret inspired by the way you were praying. I want to confess that I am seriously touched by you. You have captivated my heart".

"How could it be possible? How could I, a simple village girl, inspire so tender a sentiment in a gentleman educated in the city?"

"It is a mystery of the heart. I don't know how to explain it to you."

Rosalia, hearing the confession blushed and her heart throbbed violently. The nature around seemed to her joyous and lovely, sharing her happiness.

★ ★ ★

Rosalia went down to the garden as she used to every morning, to pluck white jasmins. She treaded them in a garland with which she adorned her parted hair, gathered behind in a loose coil, which gave her a langorous look of the heroines of the love tales.

On the previous day Carlos Manoel had told her when he had seen her in that graceful coiffure surrounded by an aura-like thread of Jasmins: "This coiffure suits you marvellously, Rosalia. At first I had the impression that you were an animated figure of the frescoes of Ajanta walking towards me".

Rosalia had laughed and thanked him, pleased at the gallantry.

Carlos Manoel followed her to the garden and said to her: "Shakuntala, in the hermitage of the forest, must have been like you a friend of flowers and the nature. Short was her idyll with the king Dachanta. For me too the hour of departure has come. The king had given to the adopted daughter of the hermit, as remembrance, a ring with his name engraved on it. What will you give me, Rosalia, to remind me of you?

"I can only give you this rose of great value to me, it is my namesake. Roses, as you know, have ephemeral lives of a single morning and your memory will die, surely, with it and you will forget me."

"Believe me Rosalia, that, far or close to you, your image will live always in my thoughts and my heart."

"With the course of time we shall see. When will you come to visit us, Carlos Manoel?" she asked anxiously, with tears in her voice.

"It will be soon, if your parents allow me".

"Why not? You know very well that our house is always open to you".

Meanwhile Mrs Lidia appeared in the veranda to remind her son of the hour of departure. This reminder filled with anguish those two hearts and interrupted their short idyll.

"Now, Carlos Manoel, you know the way. Give us the pleasure of your visit some time" said Louis Bernardo, bidding *adieu*.

"I will, uncle, with great pleasure".

The departure was very painful to young lovers who hardly foresaw the eternal Song od Love.

Rosalia felt for the first time in her life an acute pain in her heart, as if a dagger of untold feeling had stabbed it treacherously.

she lost her usual *joie de vivre* and sighed every moment, saying in soliloquy: "When will you come, when?"

Her mother asked her: "What is the matter with you, my dear? Why are you sighing all the time like a widow?"

★ ★ ★

"There is nothing mother", she answered.

"It seems to me that you are sorry because you have not gone along with cousin Lidia", said Maria Isabel maliciously.

"Oh, please, don't say that, you silly girl", said Rosalia angrily.

Translated from the Portuguese
by the author